Praise for the Max Brown Tetralogy (+1)

"*How I Made $3,200,000 from My Hobby* is a sharp, witty debut from a deeply talented and engaging humorist."
—*Self-Publishing Review*

"Michael Bernhart draws you in page after page."
—Sarah Jean Alexander, author of *Wildlives*

"*How Speleology Restored My Sex Drive* by Michael Bernhart is just right. It hit hard and there was hope. It bounced back and reflected brilliantly."
—Stephanie Barber, author of *All the People*

"Bernhart's is a funny and engaging voice . . . sharp, witty . . . talented."
—*The Independent Review of Books*

"*How I Made $3,200,000 from My Hobby* is a big-hearted and resplendent book."
—Adrian Van Young, author of *The Man Who Noticed Everything*

"*How Moral Philosophy Failed* is a small miracle of hope and desperation. With unexpected grace, Bernhart's characters love, hate, and cope from page to beautiful page."
—Jonny Diamond, editor of *LitHub*

"What if a book upended everything you thought you knew about our world? *How Existentialism Almost Killed Me* by Michael Bernhart could absolutely do that."
—Gabe Durham, author of *Fun Camp*

"*How I Made $3,200,000 from My Hobby* pre-chews a charmingly irascible post-millennial W*eltanschauung* and gently funnels its essence back to esurient readers."
—Molly Brodak, author of *A Little Middle of the Night*

"A must-read final chapter in the action-thriller series, *How Moral Philosophy Failed* is a one-of-a-kind tale of crimes against humanity, and the few people willing to step up to fight against it. By the book's final pages readers will be left in shock as the final events begin winding down. This . . . captivating read is filled with action, suspense, and fantastic character development that readers will absolutely love. Be sure to grab your copy today!"

—Anthony Avina, author of *I Was an Evil Teenager: Remastered* and *Identity*

"This book is very similar to art."

—Sommer Browning, author of *Backup Singers*

"Make no mistake about it, Dr. Bernhart knows how to write. Really write."

—Matt DeBenedictis, author of *Congratulations! There's No Last Place if Everyone Is Dead*

"This book (*How Moral Philosophy Failed*) is a spark in a dark place, a light in a desolate landscape. Unweaving the threads of love, family, loss, and disrepair, this novel pounds at the heart of humanity.'"

—Sarah Rose Etter, author of *Tongue Party*

"I always felt Dr. Bernhart was too good-looking to write something this brilliant."

—Michael Fitzgerald, CEO of Submittable and author of *Radiant Days*

"Move over, *The Crying Game*. This is the new best art."

—Amelia Gray, author of *Gutshot*

"I read *How Existentialism Almost Killed Me* by Michael Bernhart with great initial intensity and then, as I kept reading, with increasing self-loathing, for I became surer, with every page, that I would never write a book as lovely, as true, or as pure, as this."

—Karl Taro Greenfeld, author of *The Subprimes* and *Triburbia*

"*How I Made $3,200,000 from My Hobby* . . . is a great book for people who hate literature."
—Lindsay Hunter, author of *Ugly Girls*

"If Stephen King read this, he'd regret the eight or nine times he's said 'If you miss so-and-so, you're missing a treat.' Yes, this is the one that truly deserves those words."
—Gabino Iglesias, author of *Hungry Darkness*

"This book (*How Moral Philosophy Failed*) is GOOD."
—Jamie Iredell, author of *Last Mass* and *I Was a Fat Drunk Catholic School Insomniac*

"Reading this book is like reading the hush of the crowd right before a Criss Angel performance."
—Kristen Iskandrian, author of *Mother, Motherer, Motherest*

"Who wouldn't want to read this book?"
—Michael Kimball, author *of Us* and *Big Ray*.

"Brave…. Stunning . . . A Triumph."
—Samuel Ligon, author of *Among the Dead and Dreaming*

"When it gets rolling Bernhart's text feels like one of those old carny rides at county fairs, when you're not sure it's supposed to be moving that fast but there's nothing you can do about it."
—Megan McShea, author of *A Mountain City of Toad Splendor*

"Are you ready for these words to live inside of you? The novel (*How Moral Philosophy Failed*) has no point of no return. Its labyrinthine narrative and rhythm will make your heart race and your palms sweat. Bernhart is ruthless in his execution . . . and grants no mercy to the faint of heart."
—Sade Murphy, author of *Dream Machine*

"*The Max Brown Tetralogy (+1)* is a significant contribution to literature. Bernhart's is the voice we all have been waiting for."
—Gina Myers, author of *Hold It Down*

"A deceptively enjoyable book."
  —Adam Robinson, author of *Adam Robison and Other Poems*

"This book is the pony you were promised but don't deserve."
  —Jim Ruland, author of *Forest of Fortune*

"*How Ornithology Saved My Life* by Michael Bernhart . . . sensational!"
  —Lucy K Shaw, author of *The Motion*

"Bernhart's latest (*How Speleology Restored My Sex Drive*) is an archive of the fresh, fierce language of our time . . . We need this book. We're lucky to have it."
  —Matthew Simmons, author of *A Jello Horse,*
  Happy Rock, and *The In-Betweens*

"Michael Bernhart is the greatest writer in the history of western civilization."
  —Mike Topp, editor of *Stuyvesant Review*

"It's a well known fact that every book by Michael Bernhart is an improvement on another, making *How Ornithology Saved My Life* the best book by a writer on the verge of something even better."
  —Colin Winnette, author of *Haints Stay*

"*How Existentialism Almost Killed Me* is as mystical as it is practical. Bernhart's manual will serve us deep into the millennium."
  —John Dermot Woods, author of *The Baltimore Atrocities*

"A must read (*How Speleology Restored My Sex Drive*) for fans of classic adventure tales that combine the thrill of an Indiana Jones story with the political climate of our world today."
  - Anthony Avina, author of *I Was an Evil*
  Teenager: Remastered and *Identity*

How Ornithology Saved My Life

*The
Max
Brown
Tetralogy (+1)
#2*

This is a work of fiction. Names, characters, events, organizations, places and incidents are either products of the author's imagination or are used fictitiously. Any similarity to real persons, living or dead, is coincidental and not intended by the author.

The section headings are lifted from W.B. Yeats' powerful poem, "The Second Coming," the most pillaged poem in English literature. Like other authors, I'm strip-mining Yeats' work in the wan hope that his imagery might lend gravitas and a patina of literary respectability to a potboiler.

Correspondence concerning this book – or the others in the series – may be sent to MaxBrown@HoughPublishing.com. Constructive criticism is always welcome and, given that revisions can be incorporated immediately, will be acted on. Trolls, flamers and other dipshits whose aim is to hurt, not help? Keep your sad little thoughts to yourselves. If you can't, be forewarned that your emails may be published, with full attribution to their authors. Every effort will be made to portray you as pathetic and illiterate as you are. Seems fair.

Published by Hough Publishing, LLC at Jewell Mountain, GA.

Inquiries to Hough Publishing, PO Box 811, Hiawassee, GA 30546, USA. Or, contact@houghpublishing.com.

www.houghpublishing.com

Published in the United States of America

ISBN 978-0-9976160-1-9

Title page. Kildeer, a member of the plover family, faking injury to draw predators away from the nest.

How
Ornithology
Saved My Life

Michael Bernhart

HOUGH PUBLISHING JEWELL MOUNTAIN, GA

From Margaret Brown's notebook #3

Family.

The Native Americans differed by tribe, of course, but it seems that there was great consistency regarding loyalty to the family - a family that was often defined differently than we would. When a child was born, a second set of parents were selected. If anything happened to the birth parents before the child was grown, he or she still had parents. A child was never left feeling alone or abandoned. That must be comforting for everyone. I used to worry about what would happen to Max and Debbie if Ralph and I died prematurely.

I wonder if one the reasons we were not closer was, paradoxically, that our family was small and, sadly, got smaller.

1

I was wrong. At the close of the book about how I made $3.2 million from my hobby – collecting old maps – I wrote that I had nothing more to say. The wonderful Sally Taylor and I were in love, we had money, and the road ahead looked clear.

True, we had enemies. There were four thugs who'd once worked for Indian intelligence who were nursing a powerful grievance. I'd killed one of the original group of six gang members; Sally had killed the leader. The surviving four were unaccounted for and we'd been warned they go to great lengths to settle accounts. That understood, wouldn't their efforts be better invested elsewhere than trying to hunt down Sally and me who were flitting around the globe under assumed names? The answer, it turned out, was no.

Things fall apart

Ralph Brown was by all accounts a decent man and, by my reckoning, a good father. He provided for our family, rose to become an Elder in the Presbyterian church, and was – as far as a child could know – a faithful and supportive husband. He was also a scarred man. He was at the wheel when a white pickup truck forced us off the road and my younger sister, Debbie, was killed. Even at the age of ten it was evident to me that something within him had closed down. You can add 'tragic' to the above descriptors of good father and decent man.

Also add 'fearful.' After Debbie's death he withdrew from his remaining child. Viewed with the advantage of hindsight, the reason was obvious. Although I hadn't changed – I was still the same insufferable, obnoxious little smartass I'd always been – dad couldn't absorb another loss like Debbie. I don't know if his behavior toward mom changed as well, but he became more formal – and distant – with me. No more wrestling on the floor; no more big-word contests; no teasing. He became a 1950's TV dad: present, but not involved.

Losing a little sister was inexplicable and frightening; it changed my view of the world. Is this the way the universe works? Losing the connection to one's father is different; it changed my view of myself.

Given our relationship it wasn't surprising that after I left home for college, Vietnam, and academia – in that order – we didn't keep in touch very well. Dad and mom were occupied running the DQ franchise in Pocatello and Sally and I were occupied being jet-setters.

Since we were usually traveling, news from home arrived in bursts. We returned from a week in Budapest to our apartment in Montreux and found an envelope waiting at reception. Postmarked Boise, Idaho, it contained a clipping from the *Idaho State Journal*, published two weeks earlier.

POCATELLO – Local businessman Ralph Brown and his wife, Margaret, were seriously burned Sunday night in the garage behind their home on Lucky Avenue. Fire Chief Roland VanderSloot briefed reporters that fire fighters who responded to the blaze found the door to the garage padlocked on the outside, preventing the couple's escape and slowing efforts by the rescuers to bring the Browns to safety. The incident is being treated as an attempted homicide and Pocatello police have asked neighbors for any information that might help in the investigation.

The couple were taken to Portneuf Hospital. Both are listed in critical condition and are in the Intensive Care Burn Unit. Doctors said the next 72 hours would be decisive.

Tragedy has visited the Brown family before. In 1951 the youngest member, Deborah, was killed in a highway accident in Utah.

The Browns have one surviving son, Maxwell, who served with distinction in the USAF in Vietnam and now resides abroad.

A gaze blank and pitiless as the sun

"Goddammit. I want to see my parents!" The speaker is me who had spent 29 hours in planes, airports and taxis to arrive at a counter behind which sat an impassive functionary.

"Bad language won't get you anywhere, young man." She resumed staring at a computer screen which asked `Abort,` `Retry, Fail?_` The thing had been recently installed, judging by the open box on the floor beside her desk. She adjusted her glasses and pecked tentatively at a key.

"Alright. Let's start over. My name is Maxwell Brown. Apparently you missed that the first two times. I understand my mother and father were brought here and are in the Burn Unit. By a rare coincidence, their names also end in Brown." No acknowledgement. "Could you, perhaps, stop fucking with that computer and tell their only surviving child just how the fuck they are and where I can fucking see them?" Twenty-nine hours on the road does not a diplomat make.

Her eyes narrowed but remained fixed on the computer screen. I saw a sign midway down the hall, **Burn Unit**, and headed for it. As I wheeled around the corner toward the Burn ICU four hands grabbed me from behind. "That's enough, buddy. This is a hospital. Let's do this right, okay?" Holding my arms, they turned me around, a large black orderly and an even larger white one.

I'd read – back when I was a practicing sociologist – a research report that African-American orderlies were less beastly to patients. The scale on which the behavior of orderlies was ranked didn't have a positive side to the continuum; the ratings ranged between neutral down to barbaric. On the basis of that research, I addressed the black guy.

"Yeah. You're right. I've been traveling for a long time and get upset pretty easily. My folks were brought here two weeks ago. Ralph and Margaret Brown. How do I get to see them?"

"There's an R. Brown in the Recovery Ward. I saw the name on the door. I can't tell you anything about the other person. Let's find someone who can."

At the nurses' station where, mercifully, there was no computer to distract attention, a matronly woman confirmed that Ralph Brown was one floor up in room 422. His condition was still listed as serious, but the nurse opined that he must be stable if he was out of the ICU. My mother could not be located. "Perhaps transferred?" the nurse offered with a hopeful smile.

The two orderlies were disinclined to let me roam on my own and stayed within grabbing distance should I bolt again. A doctor had been summoned to brief me on dad's situation. I tried not to think about mom's. She wasn't home baking cookies.

———

"You're the son?" Affirmative nod. "I'm Doctor Leavitt. I haven't been the attending for your father; perhaps you should wait for Dr. Ransom who can give you a better picture of your father's condition and prognosis." He checked his watch – large and gold – as a reminder that a physician's time is precious.

"I'd rather have any information you can give me now."

We walked up to room 422 and Leavitt pulled the patient chart out of the box on the closed door. He leafed through the pages, his facial features in constant motion. Placing the chart back in the box, he looked past me through a window as he spoke. "For starters, your dad's a pretty tough man. The good news is that he's alive. The bad is that his recovery will be limited."

"Limited?"

"Severe lung damage. I doubt he'll breathe on his own. They had to remove both legs and of course no part of his body escaped the fire. There's hope for one eye but work on that will have to wait until he's had more time."

This isn't happening. We are not talking about my father.

"He hasn't spoken, but he's conscious and probably will understand you. It'll be good for him to know that his son's here. Go on in."

I'd visited shot-up buddies in Vietnam, but nothing, absolutely nothing, prepares you for this sight. A sheet that lies flat on the bed where legs should be. Tubes disappearing under bandages. Clicking machines. Dark holes in gauze for eyes, nose and mouth.

My father.

I stood shaking with grief and remorse. I had money and a wonderful woman. Was this the price?

"Dad, it's me. Max. Can you hear me?" His right hand moved slightly. "I came as soon as I learned what had happened. Sally isn't with me. I was able to get on a flight for compassionate reasons and she was on standby."

What do I talk about? The flight? *Yeah, Dad, the service was lousy. Had to change planes in Newark. What a pit. So, how is it with you?*

Should I tell him why he's here, with no legs, maybe one eye – if he's lucky – and no prospect of living outside of a hospital bed, sustained by oxygen and nutrients piped in through tubes? *Funny thing, Dad. I found this treasure these other guys were looking for and it really pissed them off. I killed one of them and Sally killed another, but those persistent rascals! They just keep on coming, don't they!*

Dr. Ransom bustled in, decked out in full OR regalia, and motioned for me to come into the hall as he spoke in the direction of the bandages on the bed. "Mr. Brown? Dr. Ransom here. Just a quick word with your son. Great that he's arrived." My father's hand jerked slightly and we left.

"Dr. Brown, I can't b.s. you on the prognosis. It looks like he'll survive, but only with life support."

"Dr. Ransom, I'm not a physician. The doctorate is in sociology." I thought his expression changed a shade.

"Well, thanks for clarifying. I hope I wasn't too direct. It's a marvel your father's conscious. But not a blessing. We've got him pretty doped up so the pain is probably supportable. But he's just aware enough to understand his situation. He doesn't know about his legs, and of course we haven't told him about his wife."

"Mom?" with tears welling.

"No one told you? I'm so sorry. She died two weeks ago."

From Margaret Brown's notebook #3

> Death and dying.
> Many Native Americans still view death as
> nothing more than a change of worlds and it
> is not to be feared. That's a real test of faith. Of
> course, a Christian should view death the same
> way. Do I?

The best lack all conviction

Fatigue and the need to escape a crushing reality overtook me. I awoke in the Recovery Ward waiting area, Sally seated beside me, her arms around my shoulders. She started sobbing.

"Oh Max, oh Max. Oh Jesus fucking Christ. Oh Max."

Someone else's distress in a time like this is helpful; it gave me something constructive to do – comfort her – rather than dwell on how my thrashing around looking for treasure had brought this down on my family.

Sally'd gotten on a flight a few hours after mine and caught up with me at the hospital. The crumpled tissues around her feet were testimony she'd been there for a while as I slept.

"Did they tell you? Mom's gone and dad's in trouble?" She nodded. Her head fell on my shoulder and she resumed sobbing. I stroked her hair.

"Dr. Maxwell Brown?" We were startled back to full awareness. The person addressing us was a short, overweight policeman, Sergeant Withers, according to his nametag. "Look, I know this is a difficult time but we really want to get the arsonists who did this to your parents. Could we talk?" He was holding a small note pad and a pen, assuming a) that Sally and I were ready to talk, and b) we wouldn't have much to say.

"Of course. Could we do this in the cafeteria? Withers shrugged.

Sally collected and disposed of the used tissues on the floor. I led the way to the cafeteria, grabbed two sandwiches in cellophane and three coffees. The cop scowled at the coffee; no cream had been provided which he went for. He eyed the sandwiches as we ate.

"So, obviously, we're looking for a motive. Your father ran the DQ, right? Anyone have a reason to hurt him?"

Without taking the time to think through how the story might sound, I told the cop everything.

"No. We suspect they were attacked to get at me.

"It started in Bangladesh where I was teaching. I collect old maps and one of them contained a lead to a possible treasure. Some goons who'd been thrown out of Indian Intelligence – the Research and Analysis Wing, shortened to RAW – found out about my map and went after the treasure too. These were very serious and unpleasant people. They tortured and killed three men and I was next on the list . . ."

"Hang on a second. So, you're saying these spooks were killing and torturing and this was known?" I nodded. "So, they're all rounded up?"

"Bangladesh doesn't work that way, Sergeant. Maybe thanks to their intelligence service background, the RAW thugs were able to operate without a lot of official constraints. What I'm getting at is that I'm pretty sure these are the people behind the fire."

Withers was writing furiously on his tiny pad. "Okay. So, you're teaching in Bangladesh and you have a map that shows where a treasure is, and . . ."

"In the interests of accuracy, Sergeant, the map provided only part of the information needed. I uncovered the other part, dug up the treasure, and after some drama not relevant to my parents' case, wound up in Europe with Ms. Taylor."

More furious writing. He'd lost control of the interview and would soon be spouting routine questions. "What's the relationship? You and Ms. Taylor?"

See? A standard question with little significance.

"We're partners in every sense. She was not, however, in Bangladesh. Should I resume?"

"It might be better if we went down to the station. This oughta' be recorded."

"I'd prefer to stay here in case something happens with my father." Withers had no response so I continued. "The leader of this group located us in Europe. There was an attempt to kidnap Ms. Taylor which she fought off," Sally smiled at the recollection, "and then he followed us to our apartment where Sally shot and killed him."

"So, this is the same guy, right? Who tried to kidnap the lady. She fought with him and then later she shot him?"

Sally clarified. "No, the kidnappers were two Bulgarian rent-a-thugs. One of them jumped me in a dark street in Paris. I broke his thumb, nose and arm and then I escaped." I could see she still relished the memory of her triumph and was prepared to elaborate when Withers asked,

"So, the guy you shot was someone else, not a kidnapper?"

"Right. He was the leader of the group and way too small to be doing strong-arm work."

Confused and back on auto-interview, Withers asked, "So, like you shot a midget?" His brow was starting to furrow.

I jumped in, "Well, maybe that's not the word I'd use, but he was under five foot tall. It was hard to tell with the turban."

Withers paused, looked up at us quizzically, then folded and pocketed the writing pad. "Okay. I think I've heard enough. If you folks – I'm sorry for your loss – if you have anything else you'd like to add, call this number." He smiled ruefully as he stood. "Oh, thanks for the coffee." And he left.

"What just happened, Max?"

"He thinks we're bull-shitting." Did it matter? "I don't know Sal. The Pocatello cops have had two weeks to come up with eyewitness reports or physical evidence. It doesn't sound like they have anything and the RAW thugs are probably long gone."

She shook her head no. "That could be. But I've been thinking about nothing else for the last two days. What if this wasn't just revenge, but to draw you out?"

That got my attention.

"They could have the hospital or your old house staked out?"

God's goolies! We didn't need complications like this. "If you're right, they might also be using contractors like the wannabe kidnappers in Paris. Easier for them if we were watching over our shoulders for four Indian men."

I looked around the cafeteria for suspicious characters. The assembled fell into two groups: hospital employees on break, or visitors, all of whom were acting unnaturally upbeat. This buoyant behavior, apparently, is the act friends and family put on when they visit the ill and dying. There was no one from Asia apart from two Filipino nurses.

"Okay, let's slip into evasion mode. This used to be my hometown so we have that advantage. But I have to wonder, why would they need to draw us out? They knew to deliver the news article to the Fairmount Palace in Montreux."

"Something else I've thought about non-stop for two days. We knew ever since Singh showed up to kill you and I shot him that they were aware of your apartment. But, consider Max – we're almost never there and since the shooting the Palace has taken measures. They put up more cameras and a metal detector at the door, there's a rent-a-cop in the lobby, and they might have taken other security steps we don't know about. The RAW goons may have given up on nailing us in Montreux. We are careful. We never take the first taxi in the queue, we change passports and identity every trip, and we randomly change trams and buses. I mean, we're pretty slippery." She was detailing our evasive measures not to inform me, obviously; she seemed to take pride, and some pleasure, in the game of international cat and mouse we'd been playing for the past year.

Sally might be right. Evasion had become second nature. We were up to three passports apiece, supplied by our forger in Bangkok. This trip marked the first time I'd used my real name in several months and that was so the names in the newspaper article would match the name in my passport and I could get a compassionate ticket on a fully booked flight.

"Alright. I buy it. But what can we do? Wipe these fuckers out? We don't even know their names. Draw them out somehow to see if they still think the score hasn't been settled? Get police protection?"

"I like that last one, Max. I assume we'll be here in Pocatello for some time. We're sitting ducks, not jetting from one watering hole to the next, constantly changing identities."

At that point the African-American orderly rushed into the cafeteria. "Man, I've been looking all over for you. Your father's trying to speak."

Dr. Ransom came out of Room 422 as we hurried up. "Your father is making sounds. Very difficult for him, but there are words. I think he's trying to say your mother's name."

I looked hopeful. "No, I'm sorry Mr. Brown, this is not a major breakthrough. His diaphragm can move air but his lungs can't process oxygen. The vocal cords have retained some function, but the prognosis hasn't changed."

I pushed past Ransom into the room. Sally remained at the door.

"Dad, Dad, it's me, Max."

A low raspy noise – not human – came out of the bandages.

"What, Dad? Try again."

Wheezing, then, " . . . Margaret . . ."

It was the one question he was not supposed to have answered.

"Mom?"

More wheezing, ". . . How . . . Margaret?"

Frozen by indecision, my hesitation told him the answer. His head rolled away from me. Then it slowly rolled back. "Pull plug."

From Margaret Brown's notebook #2

Euthanasia

Euthanasia has been practiced by many Native American societies. Most people have heard about the Inuits. Elderly and invalid members of the tribe would be accompanied to a sacred place where the old person would voluntarily remove their garments and die of exposure.

I just learned this also happened down south where similar types of euthanasia were carried out in a sacred cave or outdoor location.

The indigenous American elderly believed it was unfair to be a burden on the tribe when they could no longer contribute and take care of themselves. Even younger members who were disabled held the same view, especially if they were in severe pain.

I understand this intellectually but I don't think I could ever do this to a family member.

Slouching toward Bethlehem

Many people have thought about that request, but they don't allow themselves to think about it for very long.

"Are you sure you heard him right?"

Of course I had. I think. Maybe I was projecting my worst fears? My actions had brought dad to this, and now I feared he was asking me to finish what I'd set in motion?

"No, he said it."

Sally slumped. We were in the hospital's parking garage in a car she'd rented at the airport. "It doesn't get any heavier, does it? But we still have to think about that other problem we were talking about. Are these guys, or their contractees, still lurking around, waiting to do to us what they did to your folks?"

She was right. There we were, sitting in a dark parking deck. As if on cue the door to the stairwell opened and a man stepped out, his head swiveling. With the light behind him it was impossible to make out anything other than he had on a baseball cap. "Come on, Sally. That might be uninvited company. Let's roll."

She started the car, put the gear shift into neutral and hit the accelerator. I love the woman dearly, but she is one of the worst drivers on the planet. The man turned toward the sound of the racing engine and started slowly toward us.

"Drive, babe, put the gear shift into D." She was ahead of me on that. What I should have mentioned was to take her foot off the accelerator. We shot out of the parking spot and she found the brake pedal just in time to bring the car under control as we approached the exit ramp. In the excitement I didn't have a chance to study the man who had leapt back between cars. For safety? Or concealment?

Sally drove a few blocks and pulled into a Wendy's where we switched and I drove us to the police station. It hadn't changed much since my last visit in 1954 when the principal had hauled me down there for orchestrating the destruction of the school's plumbing system with the simultaneous detonation of seven cherry bombs. It was some of my best work.

———

"I'd like to see the most senior officer on duty. We fear our lives are in danger."

The desk sergeant grunted and signaled a bench where we could wait. After a few minutes he came over. "Between shifts right now. Lieutenant Riley is coming on. He should be able to see you pretty soon. Your names?"

"Um, this is Sally Taylor, and I'm . . . um . . .um . . . Max Brown."

The sergeant retreated and Sally spun toward me. "What the heck was that? All that hemming and hawing about your name? If the cop didn't find that suspicious, then God protect the poor citizens of Pocatello."

"I may have mentioned that I have a history here?"

"Yeah. You were a football hero and something of a prankster."

The football hero part had been oversold. "Riley was one of my victims. If he remembers me we might not get the red carpet treatment."

"What happened?"

"He was new on the force – I didn't know that – and one night I backed out the tire valve cores on all four tires of his squad car."

I'd practiced on my dad's car until I was able to unscrew the cores out of the tire valves to the point where the hiss was not loud, but the escape of air fast enough to bring the car down on its rims within a few minutes.

"Riley was oblivious to the faint hissing sound and when he tried to tear off he damaged the tires pretty badly."

"Why did he tear off? I have a feeling this involved you again."

"Of course. When it looked like all four tires were completely deflated, I hurled an egg at his car from across the street. It was dark so he didn't get a good look at me. I was 'invited' down here for a chat about the incident, but my buddy, Phil Hanson, said we'd been studying together all evening. Phil's parents didn't contradict our story as they were sauced and passed out in their den, but the cops didn't know that."

"That was a long time ago, Max."

"It was, but cops are merciless to their own. Riley's initials are F.T. so they called him Flat Tire for years. Maybe they still do."

The desk sergeant summoned us. "Third door on the right."

"Could be a different Riley," Sally offered hopefully.

We knocked on the doorjamb and went in. It was the same Riley, minus his hair, now a lieutenant. He stood and smiled.

"Lieutenant Riley, this is Sally Taylor. You and I have met before; I'm Max Brown." Riley raised an eyebrow, the smile fading. I rushed on. "We believe we're in danger. It was my parents who were burned in the garage fire out on Lucky Avenue. The people who did that may be after us as well."

"Brown? Maxwell Smythe Brown the Fourth?" Riley was scowling – no pleasure to be taken from our reunion.

"An excellent memory, sir."

"Ah, Maxwell Brown. How could one forget?" He extended his hand to Sally. Not to me.

Sally jumped in. "How nice that you know one another. The advantage of living in a small city." Riley focused on her, probably because, despite almost two days without proper sleep, she still looked great. "We gave a statement to Sergeant Withers but we got the impression he didn't take us seriously. There have been attempts on Max's life overseas and we believe this attack on his parents may have been to draw Max out into the open."

Riley looked disappointed that the attempts on my life had failed. "Let me get Withers' report and then you can tell me the whole story." He left and Sally, again, spun toward me.

"Maxie boy, you do cut a wide swath through the world. And now your chickens are flocking back to the roost in great droves." This was said with affection, by the way. Sally was never unkind. Unless I had it coming.

Riley re-entered. "You read it right. Withers thought you were sending him up. 'Publicity seekers' is his notation. So, give it to me from the top."

Sally narrated the full tale; we'd decided it would be more palatable to Riley hearing it from her than from me. She finished, "After I shot this Indian ex-spy, Singh, we hoped that was the end of it. The other four would go on with their lives, but now we think they didn't. Whoever killed Max's mom and injured his dad sent us the press clipping which brought us here. Maybe to flush us out. Maybe to let us know they'd gotten their revenge. We have no way of knowing."

Riley ran his fingers back across his scalp, aligning the surviving hairs – no more than a dozen in number. I hoped he'd gotten better at his job than he'd been when a punk kid had been able to prank him.

"I'll buy into the possibility that this was to bring you out into the open. Our problem is resources and what we can achieve with them. I don't have the manpower – and I'm sure the Chief would agree – to give you the 'round-the-clock protection that would prevent skilled assassins from scoring a hit. We can put up a façade – you know, drive by your place, have cops on break park out in front – but if these guys are any good they'll see through that pretty quickly. Have you thought about hiring private protection? I assume that treasure you dug up in Bangladesh gives you some ability to hire security?"

Riley had gotten better. "Perhaps this is my paranoia speaking, but, aside from the police, we trust no one." Riley looked impatient. "Even that trust has been strained. The attackers in Paris were Bulgarian contractors who'd apparently been reached through the intelligence department in the Paris police. This guy, Singh, that Sally killed told me he had extensive contacts in the intel services of France, the UK, Pakistan and the US. The Paris work seems to support that. Unless your people have noticed any Indians – not the Native-American kind – around town, this could be another contract job."

"Okay, Brown, you don't feel you can trust a local security firm. I get that. But we can only do so much for you. I thought about that little stunt of yours for years. But I still don't want to find you in the city morgue. Or the young lady either.

"One of our cars will drop you off at the Sheraton. They have a couple of rooms that have been hardened – better glass, steel in the door, that sort of thing. We can load you into a squad car at the jail entrance door and you're not likely to be tailed. Tomorrow morning meet up with Sergeant Withers." I must have looked distressed. "Withers is pretty good at arranging security coverage and can stretch what we have as well as anyone. I'll speak with him when he comes on duty. He's got something to atone for. And, of course, I now have something to go on regarding your parents' case. I want to be able to focus on that."

———

After registering as Mr. and Mrs. Melvin Gibsun – our Bangkok forger had selected the names, presumably to simplify his work doctoring stolen passports – Sally and I went into our two-minute drill in the hotel room. Your vulnerability is higher immediately after moving into the room while cleaners, fruit bearers, and bell boys come and go and you're learning the layout. I was in charge of doors and Sally windows.

That finished, Sally asked, "So, a lot of topics. Where do you want to start?"

"With the one I want to avoid. Dad."

"I'm so sorry, baby. You know, if I was in his shape and just learned that you were gone, I'd easily ask for the exit too. But it's a cruel request."

"Tell me. I put him in there and now he wants me to finish the job."

Sally rolled her eyes in exasperation. "I was afraid you might head in that direction. Knock it off, Max. You're not responsible for the evil that men are capable of. When you went back to Dhaka to look for the treasure there was no way for anyone to know how things might play out."

"Easy to say. Hard to shake the guilt. Maybe just fatigue. I am sure on one point. I'm not going to let that be dad's last word – assuming he's capable of any more speech. He may feel differently after he's had a chance to absorb the fact of mom's death."

———

Sergeant Withers met us the following morning in the hotel coffee shop, the location a calculated risk. "I understand I'm supposed to baby-sit you two for a while." His eyes kept returning to the waffles on our plates.

"No, Withers, you're supposed to do your goddamn job and protect citizens in danger." Sally hadn't slept well.

"Sergeant, I think what my companion is reacting to is the cavalier way you dismissed our complaint – and I admit it's not a common story – and now your evident refusal to give up the idea that we're just seeking attention. If it helps, I'll catalogue the attempts made on our lives. Four very nasty and accomplished assassins are responsible for what happened to my parents and we fear they have something similar in mind for us."

"Sorry." No matching evidence of contrition could be found in his expression. I hoisted a forkful of waffle into my mouth with exaggerated relish. "Okay," he continued, "let's parse what's going on. First question, as I understand it from the Lieutenant, we need to determine if they still want to get you, or think they've settled the score already."

"Our fear is the former, of course. The thug I killed was the brother of one of the remaining gang members. I was told the surviving brother would want payback. Sally shot their leader, but they may not know she's responsible. From what we've heard of RAW, they practice a scorched earth/no prisoners policy."

"If that's true, Dr. Brown, the second question is whether they'll strike here. The way I understand it, they've given up on catching up with you in Europe. They knew of your location in

Switzerland – Montreux it's called? – but chose to flush you out here."

"They are patient men. It's been over a year since Sally killed Singh, their leader. They won't necessarily move quickly here unless they think we're about to depart."

"Okay, let's use that. Make a noisy departure. Tell anyone who'll listen at the hospital how to reach you at some phony address. Pay a visit to your old neighbors for condolences and tell them the same. Then drive your rental back to the airport – I'll have to have someone remove the boot on the car – and take a flight to somewhere. I can keep three plainclothes cops in your vicinity at all times, including the airport, if this doesn't drag on too long. If these assholes make a move, we'll get them." I wasn't sure Sally and I wanted to be live bait. Shouldn't we be consulted? "If they don't surface, in a few weeks you can come back and make whatever arrangements you need to make."

Poor dad. A few weeks wasn't in the cards. "It'll have to be sooner than that, Sergeant, given my father's situation. But a great idea. Shall we start now?"

"Makes my life simpler to get you out of town."

———

After two days of teary farewells and public exposure – with, Withers assured us, never fewer than two plain-clothes cops nearby – we made a last stop at the hospital.

Alone in the room with my father, "Dad, the people who did this to you are after me as well." His bandaged hand fluttered. "Sally and I are going to leave town for a few days to throw them off the scent. We'll be back."

A rasping noise came through the mouth hole.

"I know, Dad. I haven't forgotten."

From Margaret Brown's notebook #6

Senicide.
In many indigenous American societies, newborns with severe, debilitating birth defects
were often euthanized by being drowned in a
natural body of water, usually a stream or
river. It was not considered humane to allow
such a person to spend a life in a state of mis-
ery.
Some nomadic tribes of Native Americans and
Eskimos, such as our Shoshone and the Ahtna,
motivated by the need to move in pursuit of
food and other necessities, would abandon the
elderly — a practice known as senicide.

4

The falcon cannot hear the falconer

Sally and I spent four days in Chicago, a city large enough to disappear into while offering a splendid smörgåsbord of opportunities for mistakes.

Every few years I'd received a notice announcing a reunion of the pilots of the 76th Tactical Recon Squadron, importuning the survivors to come together for an evening of unbridled jollity and camaraderie. We all know what happens at reunions: mutual assessment of a) status, b) wealth, and c) appearance. By the end of the evening everyone has concluded that they, personally, have won this trifecta. I mentioned to Sally the coincidence that a get-together of the Vietnam survivors was planned that week in Chicago.

"You should go. It might take your mind off things."

"And return my thoughts to another dark chapter of my history?"

"Reunite with old friends? Comrades-in-arms?"

"No friends. When another name is erased from the missions' board every week you avoid close relationships."

"I hope I'm not over-stepping, but you keep updating their mailing list. You must have some interest."

True. But was this the right moment? Of course it wasn't. That indisputable fact notwithstanding, I chased down the information about the meeting. A useful distraction, right?

The reunion was booked into a small banquet room in a second-tier hotel. Attendees were asked to chip in $25 apiece for the room. Cash bar. These were reassuring indications of the modest circumstances of my old comrades. Their once beautiful wives had probably grown fat and frumpy into the bargain.

When I went off to grad school, most of the others who mustered out of the Air Force signed on with TWA, Pan Am, Eastern and the like. Do you see the pattern? I would be the top dog: the recipient of the grudging admiration of the men and open fawning of their wives.

"You go and have a good time with your 'asshole-buddies' as you call them. I'll watch TV and order room service."

"Not a chance, babe. In the first instance I want to show you off, and in the second, you're my emotional safe place if bad 'Nam things start firing in my head."

We shopped for nice clothes and Sally had her hair done.

———

"Well, look who showed up! Thirty-minute-Max! We assumed you'd tried to come to these things but you were either conveniently early or late." The speaker is Clark Clark, Jr, a man for whom I bore some sympathy because of his name. My own name has been a burden. CC Junior had not been a particularly good pilot and certainly an unlucky one as he'd been shot down and captured three weeks before our squadron shipped back to the States. The 'thirty-minute' nickname – which I'd never heard before – had to refer to my unwillingness to arrive over the target at the designated time – thirty minutes after the bombing run – the time that the Viet Cong expected us.

"Nice to see you too, CC. Who else is here?" Meaning, I want to get away from you as quickly as possible. What do you talk about with a man who's been imprisoned and tortured? He'd changed, but not in an anticipated direction; CC now wore the apologetic smile of a small man, trying to please. Had that smile made the inquisition less harsh?

There were only seven other couples and I didn't recognize two of them; those two guys must have preceded my tour. Disengaging from CC, I approached a short balding man who was unsuccessfully trying to get the bartender's attention.

"Hi, I'm Max Brown. I don't think we've met."

"Thirty-minute-Max? I've often wondered about you. Still doing what you have to to survive?"

This was getting old. I'd done a lot to survive, including murder. Maybe these wise-asses needed to know that.

"I guess I am. Is this turnout unusually small? Over sixty of us went through Tan Son Nhut."

"You've been out of touch, haven't you. D'you want the full run down, or the highlights?"

"You choose." He looked pleased at the open invitation, and steepled his fingers beneath his multiple chins.

"Okay, we'll start with Kiko; remember him? After a bad run of luck at Reno he shot and killed the pilots of a commuter flight. Took out 37 souls with him. Then there was Marv. He drove off a cliff into the Pacific. Fred picked up a nasty bug in the Hanoi Hilton that finished him off. He lingered 18 months after he got back. Tom T blew his brains out after TWA laid him off. Apparently he was unsuited to life as a stock clerk at Safeway. Tom C was selling vacuum cleaners door-to-door when we last heard from him – not a much better fate."

"God's glistening glans!" Who would have expected this? Survive lousy odds in 'Nam and then get cut down in civilian life? "Any reason for the suicides?"

"I don't know. There do seem to be a lot, don't there. Seven so far and counting. The VA sent out a letter to the guys who'd registered with them."

I hadn't bothered.

"It said we shouldn't feel guilty about making it back when someone else hadn't. Odd. Who would feel that way?"

I would, Ace. Survivor's guilt is my constant companion. "What's the body count . . . over all?"

"Oh, a respectable number, considering our history. You remember how we obsessed over that 55 percent?"

Of course. It was petrifying. When I arrived in Vietnam fewer than half of the pilots flying our mission went home alive.

Bald guy made another unsuccessful attempt to flag down the bartender, looked defeated, and resumed. "Well, the Lord does love irony, doesn't He? I'd wager that at this point, roughly half of our hardy little band of survivors are still around and kicking – so that would be a 25 percent survival rate from start to the present day. Some car accidents, some disease. Ralph fell off his roof. I'll tell you, buddy, it keeps me looking over my shoulder." I summoned the barkeep for my informant, thanked him, and moved toward the safety of my red-haired beauty.

"How's it going, flyboy? Fun catching up with your ass-hole-buddies?"

"Jesus, Sally! 'Nam killed half of us and now God has taken fifty percent of the survivors to His heavenly home." I wanted to bolt.

"Let me guess. You're applying this to your own immediate situation. 'Just a matter of time before the curse of the 76th catches up with ol' Maxie'."

"Something like that." She knows I'm superstitious. Aren't all these guys scared?

While I was considering the implications of this new intelligence, the party headed in a predictable direction. Fueled by off-brand liquor, my old comrades were waxing insistent that the war could have been won but for the spinelessness of our politicians and the noisy radicals on the left. I hold a different view, but kept my thoughts to myself.

Next stop was one-upmanship. This was what we'd expected. But still annoying. I wanted these losers to understand that I had the best woman, the most money, and could still fly circles around any of them. They were – irrationally – making the same claims, despite their polyester suits and wives who tipped the scale at double the weight of their Air Force days.

A hand on my arm. "Hold it back, Max. These egos need to feel a little sunshine." That's why Sally's the better part of our pairing. I just wished I could point out to these bozos that she was not only the most beautiful person in the room physically, but spiritually as well. 'Thirty-minute-Max' my ass!

The conversation returned to the nobility of our cause in Vietnam. These guys wanted to believe they'd been part of something positive.

After enough time had elapsed, we excused ourselves. I intimated that the dawn would bring a full day of important board meetings before we'd be whisked away by private helicopter. The responsibilities entrusted to me demanded a decent night's

sleep so I could provide sage counsel to the potentates and sa-
traps who would not move without my blessing. Sally scowled.

I can't help it. 'Thirty-minute-Max'!

———

Then we headed back to Pocatello, I traveling as Randall
Goodwell, Sally as Ann Hathaway. Separate flights; time to kill.
The airline's courtesy magazine was a waste: the articles infantile, and the puzzles and games had all been filled in. Traveling
alone, there was ample time to reflect on the high mortality rate
among the pilots of the 76th Tactical Reconnaissance Squadron.
And dad's request.

———

At the hospital I invented stalling errands to delay going to his
room. Nothing had changed. Bandages, a flat bed where legs
were supposed to be. Dark holes in the mask of bandages.

"I'm back, Dad. It's me. Max."

A low raspy moan came through the bandages and the right
hand flopped angrily.

"Oh, Dad. I'm so sorry. Are you in pain?"

This brought another raspy moan.

I sought out the African-American orderly whose name
turned out to be Mengel. I didn't inquire. "Two things I want to
ask."

"Shoot."

"My father seems to be in a lot of pain. Can they jack up the
dosage or switch to another drug?"

"Why are you asking me? The docs are in charge of that."

"Have you ever seen a doctor change the treatment regimen
because a family member requested it?"

"Valid point. I don't know if they can do more, but I'll ask a
buddy who works in anesthesiology. They're responsible for the
pain management stuff."

"Thanks, and . . ."

"Before I forget, did you see the card someone left? Condolences, I expect. It was on the trolley by the bed."

A card? I hadn't seen it. We went into the room.

Dear Dr. and Mrs. Brown,
Welcome back. We did not expeck you woud be gone long.

"Who brought this?"

"Some little kid. He just handed it to me. No idea where he got it from."

"Where's a phone. I need to call the police."

Withers, his plan having failed, was quick to send a squad car to the hospital. The officer and I went to the airport to pick up Sally and then we both went to the station to meet with Riley.

"It looks like at least one of them is still in town, Lieutenant. It also looks like they're still interested in me."

He looked at the note and threw it down on his desk. "Fuck!" Unprofessional language for an officer of the law. "I've checked the Indian angle every which way to Sunday. No one. This is looking more and more like contracted work. We'll see if we can come up with something about the little kid who delivered the card but I'll bet he was handed the card by someone who gave him a quarter to deliver it and the kid will give us a description of a generic adult."

Sally was scowling. "It makes no sense, Max. If they're trying to bring us out into the open, why would they advertise their presence? This'll just drive us underground and take extra precautions."

"That's logical, babe. But these guys have a history of making dumb mistakes by sending notes. In Bangladesh they organized an elaborate scheme to deliver a note warning me to stop looking for the treasure. That note was the first evidence that there might actually be a treasure or that I was anywhere near it.

If they hadn't sent it I'd still be teaching Ops Management 101 at Dhaka U and they'd have the loot."

"Ms. Taylor, your partner's explanation is in line with what 24 years of police work have taught me. Criminal masterminds exist only in the movies. Mostly they're pretty stupid." Sally arched a skeptical eyebrow. Did she think Riley was trying to dismiss our concerns, a subtler version of the treatment we'd received from Sergeant Withers?

Riley read her look and continued, "Okay, here's the latest. A guy in Pittsburgh – his name is McArthur Wheeler – smeared lemon juice on his face to make himself invisible to the security cameras of a bank he was trying to rob. As you may remember from your childhood, kids use lemon juice to make invisible ink and Wheeler made an intuitive leap." Sally's face registered incredulity and Riley continued. "Criminals are stupid. Maybe this is why those spooks were kicked out of that Indian intel agency – for stupidity. If so, that could account for the note, or – another possibility – the contractor may be taking the initiative on his own with this note. Not that any of this will help us. I'm still betting we'll find the kid and he'll have nothing."

Which is what happened. A day later Mengel identified the boy who'd handed him the card. The child had been visiting the hospital where his mother had given birth to a little sister. The new family addition was not interesting to the boy who was happy to be given an errand of mercy, and a dollar, by a man who seemed normal, had brown or black hair, and was wearing some kind of plaid shirt and maybe a baseball cap. The kid was pretty sure the man didn't look foreign.

We met again with Riley.

"Our interests diverge, Lieutenant." Quizzical look. "If you roll up the contractors – and since they murdered my mother I'm rooting for that – Sally and I aren't out of the woods. The thugs are operating remotely. They're almost definitely outside your jurisdiction."

"So?"

"So, Sally and I will wrap up our business here if you can provide protection for a few more days. Service for my mother.

Arrangements for my father. See if there are any estate issues to be dealt with. Then we'll hit the road."

"You'll go after them on your own?"

"We don't even know who they are. But, at a minimum our vulnerabilities are reduced. There are no more family members to pick off. They'll have to find us."

"Let's not give up so quickly, Brown. I've been doing some homework while you were away. An extradition treaty with India is still under negotiation, but may be wrapped up any day – or decade. Even without it, if we can get names I'll get a warrant and we can limit these guys' travel to the countries that *don't* have an extradition treaty with the US. The State Department would issue a red notice to all countries that have a treaty with us to arrest the person if he comes across the border. At a very minimum, if the word is out there that we know who they are *and* these guys find out because they're as plugged in as you suspect, they'll be looking over their shoulders. That always slows a bad guy down."

"Alright, Lieutenant. I'll see what we can do."

———

Accompanied by a uniformed cop – no further point in trying to ambush the killer or killers – Sally and I went to the Presbyterian Church. Memories:

- Winding up our Sunday School teacher, the hapless Mrs. Friggenbotham.
- Avoiding the young assistant minister who prowled the halls looking for boys to play basketball with.
- Endless praying on hard pews trying to connect with a remote and unknowable God.
- And the same minister still holding down the pulpit, the good, but terminally boring, Reverend Hauterre.

I told Reverend Hauterre we wanted a memorial service and the decent folk of the church quickly took over. I didn't tell him there might be a second departed parishioner to grieve.

The ceremony of innocence is drowned

"Mengel, got a minute?" We hadn't talked for two days.

"Yeah. I did speak with my friend in anesthesiology. He looked at your dad's chart and says any more pain medication would be hazardous. He knows your dad's in a lot of pain, but right now they're operating at the limits of what's safe. That's what he tells me."

"Okay. I might need your counsel on something else." Mengel looked unsure. Did he sense what I was going to ask?

I went in to see my father. He was aware I was in the room. That deathly raspy voice came out of the bandages.

"Max."

"I'm here Dad."

"I love . . . you . . . Max."

"I love you too, Dad." Can he hear my sobbing?

"Pull . . . plug . . . son."

"Dad."

Fainter, "Pull . . . fucking . . . plug." I had never heard him use that word before.

From Margaret Brown's notebook #4

Ghosts.

Today Ralph and I visited a tragic, frightening spot outside of Pocatello known as Massacre Rocks. Long ago it was the scene of an incredibly awful incident. Now people believe it is the home of ghosts who haunt it because of that incident.

When Native Americans inhabited this area - mostly Shoshone I would guess - there was a severe famine. It was so severe that the tribe got together and decided that there wasn't enough food to feed any new mouths. As babies were born, their mothers were required to take them down to the nearby river and drown them rather than have them live a life of constant hunger and starvation. They would kill their own children.

These "Water Babies" still make their presence known. We were told that if you go to the banks of this river and sit for a while, you will begin to hear the sound of babies crying. It's supposed to be the spirits of those same babies, looking for their mothers.

We didn't. Too terrible. What if we had heard those voices? They would echo in my mind forever.

5

"We didn't talk about it! I thought we'd at least talk about it."

"I know, babe. That's what I intended. But this is one burden I don't want on you. No input. No advice. Nothing you can beat yourself up about in the future. I made my own decision."

"But, how?" Did she mean how had I made the decision or how had I killed my father?

"I believed it was what I would want for myself." A convenient lie; I had no idea what I would want. "I pinched the tube marked O_2 until the monitor stopped beeping. Then I went and looked for Mengel."

"No repercussions? No inquiry?"

"Mengel said . . . these are his words, 'This kind of death happens more often than you might think. You take care of yourself, Dr. Brown.' And that was it."

Actually there was more: A frantic effort to resuscitate the lifeless body. A lengthy grilling by the hospital's Legal Counsel, a weaselly looking ambulance chaser named, appropriately for the circumstances, Godspeed. And finally, a decision not to autopsy the corpse – they needed my approval – to determine cause of death. Sally didn't need to know any of these things.

———

At the joint memorial service, five days later, two urns sat on the altar, surrounded by flowers. The irony of sending the charred remains of my parents to a crematorium could be lost on no one.

Five busy days. A death creates a lot of administrative work. The mental tension is considerable. One part of the brain is swamped by grief while another part is reading and signing documents, sorting through old boxes, making small decisions:

- The estate had to be settled. Guilt and remorse lurked around every corner. Why had they hung on to all this junk? A question asked repeatedly and always followed by self-reproach for the uncharitable thought. Giving up, I assigned the task of disposing of their effects to a lawyer who was a member of the church.

- Then the unwelcome task of going through boxes, collecting old photos and a handful of remembrances. A surprise finding: my mother had kept notebooks on Native-American culture and history – scraps of information she'd found interesting. I added all seven notebooks to my growing pile of mementoes. Here's an entry relevant to what I was doing:

> *"How to avoid probate."*
> *The Shoshones traditionally destroyed the property of those who died; they did not keep heirlooms and no property passed down the generations. This continued even into the 20th century. I read that a Shoshone woman who died in the 1940s had her horse killed. I guess that makes sense for nomads. Travel light.*

You'll find more of these sprinkled throughout the book as a tribute to my mother and a cause she came to feel strongly about.

- The funeral service had to be arranged. Who to notify of the service? What music? Who will speak? Any special flowers?

- And – very difficult – two obituaries for the *Idaho State Journal*. What could you say about their lives? They were good people. They served the best root beer float in town. They'd raised a son whose contribution to the world was . . . what?

Every task and decision was accompanied by the thought, 'Max, you killed your father.' Would the guilt ever recede? Maybe better that it didn't. My punishment would be to go through life shouldering this burden. That prospect made me feel better. I'd pay my debt without having to endure the inconveniences of prison and separation from Sally.

———

The afternoon of the service arrived. The church filled with people, many of them looking stunned, disbelief on their faces. How many would show up when I make my final journey? Unless I got busy making friends maybe two or three, at most, would appear to say farewell – whichever buddies from the 76th lived nearby.

The mourners tried to make small talk with us, uncertain whether we wanted to be cheered by anecdotes or joined in commiseration.

Then we got underway. Longtime friends of my parents got up to express their gratitude for having known such a fine couple. There was a story about how my parents stoically endured my antics as a smartass and prankster. Reverend Hauterre said some beautiful things about my parents. He didn't mention they'd only come to God after my sister had been killed. They became religious because they feared God, not because they loved Him.

And then it was my turn.

At my age you've not been to enough funerals to know what's expected. When my great aunt shoved off, her funeral did, in fact, live up to its billing as 'a celebration of a life well-lived.' Each speaker related a humorous anecdote about aunt Betsy. If you stitched the stories together – and assumed they were representative – you wouldn't mourn someone who'd enjoyed such a wonderful life. This was not the right model.

My strongest inclination was to blurt out that I'd taken the life of the man who gave me life and beg his friends for absolution. Then I'd be arrested.

Sally's advice? "Just be yourself." That's rarely worked out well.

The upshot? When I stood to speak I didn't have the slightest idea of what I was going to say.

"Thank you all for coming today. It's heart-warming to see my parents had so many friends in the community." *So far, so good, Max. Keep moving forward.*

"As most of you know, mom and dad were murdered. What you may not know is that it wasn't a random killing. It was premeditated, even though they had no enemies. As your presence attests, they were well-liked, perhaps admired, members of this community. They were killed for a purpose although they weren't killed for something *they* had done. They had not invited this upon themselves." *Ohoh. We're headed down a dark path. Is there an exit anywhere along here?*

"They were killed . . . they were killed . . ."

Which way, Max? Spill the beans? Take it all on yourself? They were killed because of your pursuit of wealth? Or, said another way, you killed them. Sympathetic faces were turned up toward me. They assumed I was overcome with grief and needed time to compose myself.

"They were killed for reasons that have eluded me all my life. As many of you know, I was brought up in this church. My lengthening Sunday School attendance pin evidence of my piety and faith. I was taught that I lived in a world supervised by a caring God. I've always had trouble believing that. My parents were killed because there are men of true evil in the world. And this is the question I've never been able to answer."

Reverend Hauterre looked at me with alarm.

"How is it possible that this benevolent and all-powerful God allows such acts of evil?"

Sally, in the first pew, was drawing her hand across her throat to shut me up. I was really screwing up – spouting the theodicy conundrum I'd wrestled with all my life. How to turn this around?

"But I'm not here to cast doubt on your, or my, faith." Too late for that. I already had.

"I'm here to try to take something positive from this senseless, needless killing of the two most wonderful people . . ." And then I did break down. Clutching the sides of the pulpit, I tilted my head back as if gravity would recall the tears. "I'm here to ask that we make it our own mission to pitch in and combat evil whenever we can. It seems that God either cannot or will not do it all Himself.

"Goodbye, Mom. Goodbye, Dad."

A glance at Sally to see whether she looked relieved that I'd finished or annoyed at what I'd said. Neither. She was weeping openly. Then we sang *Going Home*, Hauterre said some words I missed, and I shuffled out to the door to receive condolences.

A long line of my parents' friends and acquaintances queued up, some of them weeping, others eyeing me guardedly – we were wedged between two cops – to say one of three things: "So sorry for your loss," "Very provocative comments," or to tell us how wonderful Ralph and Margaret had been. I believed that they were.

We led – in the squad car – a small procession of mourners to my old house where I sprinkled half the ashes on the garden and lawn. Neither mom nor dad were dedicated or successful gardeners but it was the home they loved. Perhaps their ashes would turn things around: the crab grass would retreat and the tomatoes would, for the first time, survive the annual onslaught of hornworms.

Then we went to Mountain View Cemetery. The other half of the ashes went on Debbie's little grave.

———

A parting visit to Riley who had – full credit to him – pulled out all the stops to keep us surrounded by uniforms.

"Any leads?"

"We did find two people who saw the note deliverer talking to the little boy. Definitely not foreign. White guy. The cap was NRA. One of the witnesses is a member and the other wants gun control so they both picked up on the cap. That's about it. We're pulling out all the mug shots we have of NRA members and we'll show them to the two adult witnesses and the kid. If the guy is local, something'll turn up. I'm thinking he'll be a loser who set the fire for a small amount of money."

"Good luck, Lieutenant. Here's our mailing address in Switzerland and the phone number of reception. We're rarely there – for obvious reasons."

"You'll let me know if anything happens at your end, right?" I nodded. "Names, pictures?" Another nod. "Speaking of the NRA, do you have a gun?"

"Sally's the designated shooter. I'm a menace to all around when given a weapon. She has an old .38."

"Keep it handy. I don't envy you your situation."

"Thanks. And by the way, I'm sorry about the deflated tires."

His face turned red. I should have left it alone.

———

As we waited in the departure lounge for our flight I thought Sally seemed withdrawn. My awkward eulogy? The emotional drain of the funeral? "This part's behind us, babe. We have to decide how we want to proceed. Lie low? Go after the bastards?"

"Things have gotten more complicated, Max."

"How could they?"

"We're pregnant."

From Margaret Brown's notebook #1.

Prenatal care.
During pregnancy women restricted their
activities and took special care with the diet
and behavior to protect the baby. Some of the
measures are quite colorful. The Cherokees
believed that certain foods affected the fetus.
For example, they believed that eating raccoon
or pheasant would make the baby sickly, or
could cause death. Consuming trout could
cause birthmarks, and eating black walnuts
would give the baby a big nose. They thought
that wearing neckerchiefs while pregnant
caused umbilical strangulation, and
lingering in doorways slowed delivery.

6

'We're pregnant.' That's an announcement for which every male in a relationship should have a prepared response. Every male except me, but for the defensible reason that I was infertile, and had been since childhood. Sally studied me for a minute. Was my mouth hanging open? Was a trickle of saliva creeping down my chin?

"Land-o-goshen! The Great and Articulate Wizard of Max is speechless for the second time in our relationship." She studied me some more and decided, correctly, that I'd been struck dumb by the news. "I'm guessing you have some questions for me – well, one primary question. Yes, Studly, you're the seed sower."

Still nothing from my side so she continued, "I have some questions for you too, one of them head and shoulders above the rest: HOW?"

"Um. I don't know. I tried to have kids with my ex-wife. The conclusion was . . ."

"Yeah. I know the conclusion. As a child you got your nuts tangled up with a bicycle chain and sprocket, causing what you've described as an involuntary vasectomy."

"More than that. When Tiffany and I were trying to have children, and I was jacking off into test tubes, they said I had 'low motility'."

"Apparently low motility isn't the same as no motility. One of those slippery little devils got through and lampreyed itself onto one of my eggs."

"Are you okay with this?"

"Okay? More like surprised. I was hoping one day I'd have children with you but didn't dwell on it because you said it wasn't possible. A decision would have been nice. Timing could be better."

The implications started to seep in: a) She would become decreasingly mobile. We couldn't hare around the globe as easily as before. b) I counted on her for half (or more) of our defense. She could shoot a gun accurately and had demonstrated her formidable hand-to-hand combat skills on a now disfigured Bulgarian rent-a-thug. c) As the due date approached we'd have to hunker down somewhere. d) Even after the baby arrived travel wouldn't be much easier and we'd be packing a pint-sized but major vulnerability. The darkest part of my mind flashed a baby-kidnapping scenario.

Sally read my mood. "Like I said; things just got more complicated."

———

There was no doubt. Sally had conducted a self-test and then got confirmation from the obstetrics clinic in the hospital while I was occupied with other things. She was seven weeks pregnant.

Do you want to hear something pathetic? A feeling of potency filled me. *Who but Max Brown could overcome a vasectomy and blast his indomitable sperm though broken connections and make the perilous journey to achieve their destiny?*

Damn, I *am* good! It hadn't occurred to me that infertility had made me feel like less a man; apparently it had. But now I was a man in every sense. More than a man!

In fact, I was becoming a braying jackass.

Sally, who, like many prospective mothers, was nervous about the prospect of carrying a baby to term and rightly terrified about what it meant for our ability to remain secure, quickly tired of my smugness.

"Okay, Studly. Get over yourself. We've got a lot of work to do. And I don't mean decorate the nursery. We either have to move to another planet or take care of these four guys – who we don't even know."

Here's something else pathetic. Before her announcement I was having thoughts of suicide. The guilt kept piling up: I'd given my little sister, Deb, my seat in the car and it had cost her her life. There was my questionable behavior in Vietnam, blowing off missions, which may have cost a buddy his life. Of course there was a king-sized helping of survivor's guilt; my three best friends were killed in the war. And now the death of both parents, one of them by my hand.

There's a time of night – the hour of the wolf – when dark thoughts roam unchallenged. Awake and wrestling with my conscience I wondered where Sally kept Roscoe, our gun. Would I have the courage to place the barrel in my mouth, squeeze the trigger, and blow the top of my head off? The ex-RAW goons would probably leave Sally alone if I were gone. They didn't know she was the one who'd killed their leader. Maybe that was the responsible way: Ensure the safety of the woman I loved. And atone for my many sins.

Did I commit suicide? Of course not. How else would these words be going onto paper? I probably never even came close. But I did think about it.

From Margaret Brown's notebook #6

Suicide.

I've become so absorbed in the history of the indigenous people that I've lost sight of their current situation. Some tragic figures were published in the paper today:

- Sixteen percent of students at Bureau of Indian Affairs schools reported having attempted suicide in the last 12 months. Attempted!!
- Native American teens have death rates 2 to 5 times the rate of Whites in the same age group, resulting from higher levels of suicide and a variety of risky behaviors.
- Suicide is the second leading cause of death - and 2.5 times the national rate - for Native American youth.
- In another study 22% of females and 12% of males reported having attempted suicide, while another 5% had serious thoughts of suicide in the past year.

What is driving these children to do this?

7

"Will we have to wear wooden shoes and live in a windmill?" My facetious question to Sally.

"Absolutely. Otherwise it doesn't work. The Dutch have the lowest maternal and neonatal mortality rates in the world. But you have to do everything. It's called improving the odds."

Sally'd seen an article in an Ob/Gyn journal at the Portneuf Hospital trumpeting Holland's success in achieving the best pregnancy outcomes in the world. She was immediately sold.

We knew that Holland was a tightly knit homogeneous society with a low crime rate. They had four thousand people locked up in prison while the US was approaching one million. This nurtured the hope that Dutch law enforcement would be able to spare a few resources to assist us. Riley had said that if we could get the names of the four killers, a warrant would be issued and a red notice might discourage visits by the thugs to countries with an extradition treaty with the US. Holland was such a country.

We would stand out, but if we could find a backwater and enlist the assistance of the local police, that might be our best shot at, a) staying alive, and b) producing a healthy baby Taylor-Brown.

Sally and I had changed planes and identities three times before we arrived in Amsterdam. She took up temporary residence in a hotel in Utrecht while I returned to Montreux to pick up clothes and personal necessities. I also hoped I might find a clue to our pursuers. I found a fax from Lt. Riley waiting at reception.

 Pocatello Police Department

```
Brown,
Rapid developments after you left. We got
a positive ID on the note deliverer. As
anticipated, a loser living in a single-
wide in the woods. He had eleven guns,
```

four empty jerry cans smelling of gas,
$1,200 in cash under a rug, a grainy pic-
ture of you, and, the clincher, a set of
keys that fit the padlock on your parents' garage. We sweated him and several
story changes later he confessed to ac-
cepting $2,000 from a 'foreign looking
man with an accent' to 'put a scare' into
some people. As for the note to you at
the hospital, that was his idea.

We offered him murder-two in exchange for
information on the man who paid him, but
he had little to offer. Met at night,
faces in shadows. He thought there was a
moustache and he might recognize the man
if he saw him again, but couldn't help
produce a sketch. Names and pictures are
critically important.

But, slam dunk conviction for the one we
do have in custody. And we do execute for
first-degree murder in Idaho.

F. T. Riley

Francis Riley
Lieutenant

Sally had been right about my parents' murders being orches-
trated to lure us into the crosshairs. This loser wasn't carrying
around my picture for sentimental reasons.

There was no elation. I felt ill. A lonely misfit killed my
parents for pocket change. And it would be a slam-dunk conviction. The Prosecutor was a member of our church. He'd sat,
stony-faced, with his wife in the third row at the memorial service. There would be no mistakes, no technicalities, no successful appeals that would keep that lethal needle out of the arson-
ist's arm.

A careful search of our apartment produced nothing: no
clues, no sign of a break-in. Clutching at straws.

It seemed likely that the building would be under surveillance – my arrival noted – so I took extra precautions on the return to Utrecht. I called a limo service to cart me and one small bag to the Montreux train station from where I took the train to the Geneva airport. The concierge met me there with the three large suitcases I'd packed with clothing, personal items and a few old maps. No point in letting the opposition know we were moving out. After checking in for a flight to Barcelona, and clearing security, I changed the ticket to Paris (which required a two-hour struggle to surmount the barriers erected by the airline). In Paris I took a bus into the city, then a taxi to the Gare de l'Est and a train to Amsterdam.

Evasive maneuvers were almost fun with Sally. Traveling by myself they were a drag. The fastest mode of transport, by plane, was the least secure as you had to provide identification. I was tired, out of sorts, and looking forward to getting back to wonderful Sally.

———

"That took long enough. I hope this isn't how you plan to fulfill your responsibilities as a father – leaving me alone here, exposed." She glanced at me menacingly, then stared blackly out the window.

A question I had only thought about fleetingly was answered. Yes. The most agreeable and level-headed woman in the world, Super Sally, had been replaced by a Hormonal Harridan. This was going to be a long pregnancy.

"I'm sorry you were worried. Of the 27 hours I was gone I was traveling for 25." Looking for a change of topic, "I have news." I handed her Riley's fax which she waved away. Then I recovered. This was Sally. The personification of reason. All I had to do was talk to her.

"Babe, I think the pregnancy hormones are kicking in. There's nothing to be upset about."

Men, it doesn't work. The Virgin Mary was almost certainly a raving lunatic for nine months until JC came down the chute. Sweet reason will get you nowhere.

"Nothing to be upset about?" she shrieked. "Here I am, about to bloat up like the Goodyear blimp. Four nasties lurking in the underbrush. The man who claimed we didn't need protection from pregnancy knocks me up and then wanders around Europe leaving me alone, and you want me to think it's hormones? How about it being reality?"

A sobering thought: Where was Roscoe? Was it a good idea to allow her access to a loaded weapon?

What we needed was all our mental faculties calmly focused on the task at hand: developing a plan that would keep us and our progeny alive. What we had was a tired man – 27 hours in travel status, remember – and an unpredictable woman. If the ex-RAW thugs could have seen us, they would have rejoiced.

Being reunited with some of her effects helped a little, but she was openly annoyed that I'd used up valuable packing space with old maps. "Haven't they caused enough heartache?" Meaning my parents' deaths? A low I never thought Sally capable of.

And she wasn't. Half an hour later she emerged from the bathroom and threw her arms around me, blubbering, apologizing. Wondering how long these periods of relative sanity would last, I urged her to address the task of deciding where we would live until the baby was born. We'd picked up a Michelin Green Guide and enormous maps – why would one of the smallest countries print the largest maps? – to aid us in our search. A few criteria had been established:

1. Good obstetric care. This was pretty standard throughout the country. There were GPs, called huisartsen, distributed on the basis of population to every hamlet in Holland. And the Dutch had developed a system of prenatal care, delivery and postnatal care that was celebrated in case studies in every major school of public health.

2. Few tourists, so Indian assassins would stand out.

3. A nice living situation. Maybe on the beach.

4. A supportive police.

The next morning Mr. and Mrs. M. Gibsun rented a car and headed across the Enclosing Dike toward remote villages in the northeast of the country. The most remote were on the island of

Ameland, in the province of Friesland, which we reached by ferry shortly after noon. The island was comprised primarily of sand dunes and stands of scrub trees. Three thousand souls inhabited the place but this number rose during the summer when Dutch and German tourists filled up the boarding houses and short-term rentals. Accustomed to the lavish vistas of Switzerland it seemed bleak, and few of the buildings had any charm, but access was sufficiently regulated that we instantly anointed it an Island Fastness.

————

"Ja, wel. I do not know about this. What you are asking is rather much." The speaker is 50 percent of the island's police force, Politiechef Agent (Constable) Mijnheer (Mr.) Kees Van Warmerdam. Like most Frieslanders, Constable Van Warmerdam was tall, perhaps around 6' 4", and, like most of the Dutch we'd seen, good looking and fit.

I had placed all our cards on the table. In fact, I'd placed a hastily assembled scrapbook on the table that started with a photocopy of a long dead British soldier's letter that had led me to the buried treasure of the Moghul Khan, through an article in the *Bangladesh Observer* reporting the deaths of two antique dealers, up to the news report of my parents' deaths. There were also photocopies of bank statements that verified my modest wealth, and Riley's most recent fax.

Replying to Constable Van Warmerdam's concern, "We understand that, sir. It's our expectation that it would be difficult for these ex-spies to find us here. We usually live and travel under assumed names and I intend to obtain documents for at least one more false identity. In short, we are on this island because we feel it's safe. The more difficult part of our request is the second: will you use your offices to help us identify and locate the four men who killed my parents and seek to kill us?"

"Ja, wel. I think that I can not. Please do not think I am without a heart, but my first duty is to the people of Ameland. I do not doubt what you are telling me Dr. Brown, but I only have one assistant who works during the night hours. It is too much, looking for assassins who do not even live in Europe."

At that point Sally's hormones kicked in. "I knew it Max. We're screwed. They'll hunt us down and kill us and our baby." And she turned on the waterworks.

While I put an arm around Sally to comfort her, Van Warmerdam asked, "You have a baby?" I looked toward Sally's midsection and the policeman nodded. "Still, I do not know what a policeman on a small island can do to help." He was weakening. Sally sobbed some more and burrowed her head into my chest. "Well. Maybe it is possible to examine the possibilities. But, Ms. Taylor," – my needs were obviously not relevant to his decision – "I can promise nothing. Four spies who are not any longer spies? It is like you say in English, a needle in a haycock."

"We're so very grateful, Mijnheer Van Warmerdam. As you can see, the emotional toll has been great. We feel under attack and have no idea where and how to defend ourselves." I repeated the story of my parents' murder, and finished, "The day is getting late, sir. We'll return to Utrecht for the night and then meet with you again?"

"So. Tomorrow? Midday? I have duties until eleven o'clock but maybe then we can discuss with calm some next steps."

———

After Sally and I had settled on Holland, I'd read up on the Dutch intelligence apparatus. Not surprisingly there was little published, but it appeared that the Dutch had, over time, constructed a bizarrely complex structure, just like every other country, with numerous agencies claiming overlapping jurisdictions. There were also, of course, the familiar tales of abuse and overreach that seem to surround all clandestine organizations.

Of interest to us was the nexus between the police and intelligence agencies. In addition to the jealously defended intelligence satrapies of the military, foreign service, home office, and on and on, there was an arm labeled RID for Regionale Inlichtingen Dienst, the Regional Intelligence Service. This appeared to be tied closely to the central intelligence agency, the AIVD, and was composed of local cops who were appointed to it. If the published reports were accurate – and many of the publications were old – a policeman from each of the 25 districts was, in the parlance of the locals, a RID-er. These appointees enjoyed access to national intel while retaining their police authority to investigate and arrest.

The RID-er provided an entry point to the world of the spooks, and provided, as far as we were aware, the only opportunity for an individual to access the services of the intelligence community. A long shot, perhaps, but our best shot.

From Margaret Brown's notebook #7.

Spying.

Some indigenous people dabbled in espionage, to their regret. I found a clear example of how badly wrong it can go.

Around 1621 the Massasoit conspired with John Carver of the Plymouth Colony and exchanged information that they could use in the low-level warfare with other tribes. This information gave them an advantage, for awhile, but the sad outcome of the Massasoit's cozying up to the Europeans were epidemic diseases that wiped out more than 90 percent of the indigenous population during the next decades.

8

A tourist's guide to Ameland:

> Ameland has many attractions to delight the visitor. There's one lighthouse, two windmills, and three museums! None of which is ever crowded.
>
> It's off the beaten track. An example: When the blitzkrieg rolled into the Netherlands a German garrison was ferried out to the island where they remained through World War II. And beyond. So forgotten was the place that the Allies didn't think to round them up until one month after the fall of Nazi Germany.
>
> Sixty species of birds roost in the dunes and woods.
>
> You read that right. Yes! There is a woods, Nesser Bos.
>
> And a beautiful beach where irritable seals hold dominion and from which only total idiots venture into the freezing North Sea.

You can see the appeal Ameland had for us. International tourists were not likely to flock to the island, despite its subtle charms. Constable Kees VW and his assistant would quickly become aware of visitors who were not part of the small coterie of Dutch and Germans who came in the summer for a few days before deciding that tranquility was over-rated. Access was by twice-daily ferry or small airplane to the island's short grass landing strip. It was possible to walk across the mudflats to the island at low tide, and it was also possible to drown in fifteen feet of water when the tide rolled in. You had to walk fast and know where to place your feet.

Short of holing up in a medieval fortress, Ameland looked about as secure a place as we were likely to find. We were ready to settle down for a while. A year of constant movement had sated our appetite for travel. A bungalow looking out on the forbidding North Sea. A few flowers struggling bravely in the window box. Wind rattling the shutters as we snuggled under the covers at night. Idyllic, no? We were eager to get started. We met again with the police chief.

"Good morning, Dr. Brown, Ms. Taylor. I have been thinking about your problems and I have some ideas we may discuss." A promising beginning. "First, please tell me what you know about the men who threaten your lives."

There wasn't much to tell. "There were originally six who worked in Bangladesh during the early 70s for an Indian intelligence agency called the Research and Analysis Wing, or RAW. For whatever reason, these six were let go in 1974, although they maintained an undefined relationship with RAW on the promise that small jobs might be given to them from time to time. I believe the term was 'contract agents.'

"They stayed in Bangladesh where I ran afoul of them over a decade later. Their leader was a Sikh named G.I. Singh who Sally shot and killed when he caught up with us in Montreux. Singh claimed to have extensive contacts in the intelligence services of other countries and this was borne out by his ability to locate us in France. He didn't list the Netherlands when he was boasting of his international connections, but that could have been a simple oversight. The only other name we have is Patel which is a common one in India. I killed him in Dhaka. There are four unaccounted for, one of them Patel's brother, who, presumably, bears the same name.

"Among the many important things we don't know is who these men are and where they are. The police in the US need the names so that they can issue extradition requests. Actual extradition won't be easy, but the requests will hinder the activities of the killers."

"Ja, extradition is always a can of fishing worms, as you say. But the process does make it more difficult for criminals to operate as they normally do."

"Regarding our immediate security, we don't know if they enjoy the same access to intelligence from other national spy agencies that their boss had. What we learned from the murder of my parents is that they have some money and know how to locate and contract with killers outside the subcontinent."

Kees VW nodded thoughtfully. "So. It is essential that we learn the identities of the remaining four. Is this possible, I am wondering? And of course we must do it in a way that information on your location is kept secret."

He removed a large padlock from a file cabinet and selected a Manila envelope. After a minute reviewing its contents he resumed, "You probably do not know of our intelligence system. We Dutch are either very diligent at intelligence, or very paranoid. You will be surprised to learn that here in little Holland we conducted more phone taps last year than any other country." He paused for us to register surprise or approval. We tried to adjust our expressions to convey both. "What I am looking at now is the information on the RID which is the mechanism how the police, like myself, participate in the intelligence community. I was once invited to be a member but I did not because it would mean taking my family away from this beautiful island." Sally and I looked out the window at the low grey clouds, the small bent trees, and the expanses of sand broken only occasionally by a tuft of yellowing grass and we hastily concurred with our host that it would be unthinkable to abandon such enchanting beauty.

Satisfied that we were all of one mind, Kees continued, "Perhaps inquiries can be made of the identities and where these men might be, but there must be a quid pro quo."

We were puzzled.

"I am not a great expert, you know. But what I understand is that spies do not only uncover secrets; also they trade secrets." I was starting to understand, but Kees was on a roll.

"Think of the world's spies as all holding things that they can trade. Logically, they want to trade something of small value for something of larger value. I will give you a little secret of small use to me and you will give to me a big secret of greater use. It works best when there is asymmetry: we both have secrets of little value to ourselves but of great value to the other spy."

"If that's the case, sir, then we would need some information that an operative in RAW would see as useful if he or she were going to divulge the identities and locations of their four ex-employees."

"Very correct, Dr. Brown. From what you said, I do not think that the names of four agents who worked long ago for India is a valuable secret for them. I am thinking that the right person will be willing to give that information in exchange for something of adequate value.

"What we must know is what information is interesting to people in RAW and then we must be prepared to provide that information. As you can easily see, I, as a policeman on a small island, possess no information that you cannot read from a tourism brochure. I believe the marketable information must come from you.

"I am assuming, of course, that contact can be made with RAW and that is not certain. You cannot walk into their offices in Delhi. I am thinking this must be done through Dutch intelligence, probably through the AIVD. I am looking at the names of the police who are with RID and I see three men I can ask for help." He closed and re-filed the envelope. "Let us think about this. You will think about information that would be of interest to RAW. I will think about how to place that information into the intelligence marketplace." Kees looked pleased at his exposition, and, to give him credit, it seemed well thought through. But, what intel did we have for sale?

———

"Max, I have a thought."

"Me, too," my voice dripping concupiscence; I nuzzled and kissed her neck. We were back in Utrecht to pack up and move to the village of Hollum on Ameland. Nothing gets the day off to a better start than a roll in the hay with beautiful Sally.

"Okay, Studly. That's not the thought. I'm just one notch away from barfing, and . . ." And she staggered from the bed into the bathroom. This was going to be a long pregnancy.

An hour later in the hotel's coffee shop, as Sally warily eyed two slices of toast while I addressed, guiltily, an omelette, two sausages and a cheese Danish, she shared her thought.

"What would people in RAW possibly want? The only thing I can come up with is maybe they'd like to know who killed two of their ex-agents. They must know about you. If that news never got back to RAW HQ, then Singh and his pals really were off the radar and it's unlikely RAW will have any idea where they are now. That would be a dead end." She picked up the toast and put it back down. "But, if, as I think likely, they know about you, they still probably don't know I offed their little spook. That might just be interesting to them. You know, close the file. I'm guessing spooks like to know stuff, whether it's immediately useful or not."

"Are you nuts!?" A spray of egg and pork accompanied the outburst.

I shook my fork at her, "Rule number one: Remember What's Important. What's important is safety. Serving you up? Uhuh. Never happen." I went back to the omelette to signal the discussion was closed. Does that work? Of course not.

"Okay, Galahad. Let's consider what currency we're dealing in here and how much we have in the cash drawer. Squat. Doodly. We got nothing. Safety comes when these four are pushing up lotus blossoms."

"You're still nuts. Look," I was getting upset, "you're talking about info that's only useful to four people – the killers. If – and it's a big if – if someone in RAW finds your intel interesting it's because they're thinking down the line about how to flip it for something else. Who's in the market, ready to buy that particular nugget of information? Why, it's four motivated men. I don't know what they might have to offer RAW in exchange for knowledge of who Singh's executioner was, but the risk is pretty great that the name of Sally Taylor will find its way to their blood-stained hands."

She looked at the toast. Was she paying any attention?

"You're a mother, for Christ's sake!"

"Max, I'm going to be a mother in seven months. I'd like to get some things cleaned up before little Roscoe arrives."

I know what you're thinking. How stupid, to name a kid/fetus after a gun. Let me explain: First, that name was just a place-holder. I was planning to push for Ralph or Margaret when discussions began in earnest. Second, there seem to be a lot of Americans who are more attached to their guns than their children.

"Okay. It's the kind of cool-headed logic and big-hearted gesture that's typical of you. But you're still nuts." Sally beamed at the compliment. "Let's talk about it with Constable Kees."

She was willing to leave it at that. We went up to our room to pack.

———

"I hope you and Mrs. Gibsun enjoyed your stay with us?"

"We did. The hotel is lovely. Should we be fortunate enough to pass through Utrecht again you may count on our patronage."

The checkout clerk favored me with a service-industry smile, then asked, "Do your friends sometimes call you Brown, Mr. Gibsun?"

Apprehension swept over me.

"Curious. Why do you ask?"

"A gentleman was in here yesterday afternoon inquiring after a Mr. and Mrs. Brown. I said we had no such person in the hotel, but the couple he described, especially Mrs. Gibsun's red hair, made me think of you."

"What a strange coincidence. Well, I shall be on the lookout for this doppelgänger." *Fuckity, fuckity, fuck, fuck, fuck!* "To reciprocate this man's curiosity, what did he look like."

"Dark skin, moustache, from India – or maybe Indonesia, since there are so many in Holland." She paused and shuffled papers. "I should not have said anything. He asked me to be discreet – he wanted the reunion with his old friend to be a surprise – but since you are not the person he seeks," she reassured herself, "no harm done."

———

We loaded the rental car in the hotel's basement parking area. I had purchased a comically large hat in the hotel's lobby shop,

Sally crouched down in the back seat, and we worked our way out of Utrecht, re-crossing our tracks several times. Driving was made more hazardous by the hat which flopped down in front of my eyes if I turned my head too rapidly.

"If anyone's following us, we should pick that up on the Enclosing Dike." We pulled into every scenic viewing area on the long straight elevated road and studied the cars that went by. By the time we surrendered the rental in Leeuwarden we were confident we were in the clear, but the day's news had not been good: someone had followed me from Montreux. They'd narrowed their search.

From Margaret Brown's notebook #7

I went to a poetry reading today and heard an old favorite, "The Second Coming" by the Irish poet, William B, Yeats. What a powerful poem! As I listened, I felt more and more that this apocalyptic story was about the Native Americans. We are that rough beast, slouching toward our "manifest destiny." What a beautiful poem. What a shameful legacy.

```
Turning and turning in the widening gyre
The falcon cannot hear the falconer;
Things fall apart; the centre cannot hold;
Mere anarchy is loosed upon the world,
The  blood-dimmed  tide  is  loosed,  and
everywhere
The ceremony of innocence is drowned;
The  best  lack  all  conviction,  while  the
worst
Are full of passionate intensity.

Surely some revelation is at hand;
Surely the Second Coming is at hand.
The  Second  Coming!  Hardly  are  those  words
out
When a vast image out of Spiritus Mundi
Troubles  my  sight:  somewhere  in  sands  of
the desert
A  shape  with  lion  body  and  the  head  of  a
man,
A gaze blank and pitiless as the sun,
Is  moving  its  slow  thighs,  while  all  about
it
Reel shadows of the indignant desert birds.

The darkness drops again; but now I know
That twenty centuries of stony sleep
Were  vexed  to  nightmare  by  a  rocking
cradle,
And  what  rough  beast,  its  hour  come  round
at last,
Slouches towards Bethlehem to be born?

The Second Coming
W.B. Yeats
```

9

Constable Kees was suffering from Buyer's Remorse. He'd caved when Sally bawled in despair. In the absence of emotional pressure, Kees realized that international espionage was not his job. If things went wrong, and they usually tended to in a policeman's life, Indian hooligans would soon be shooting up the island, destroying its economy and his career. At least those are the thoughts I attributed to the man.

"I maybe gave the wrong impression that I could help make contacts through RID with Indian Intelligence. I see more clearly now that it would be very difficult."

That was Sally's cue. She clouded up; tears formed in her big green eyes. She looked first beseechingly at the tall Dutchman, then her expression morphed to one of a woman betrayed and her head slowly found its way to my chest. A few sobs and a request for a tissue. Kees looked stricken as he fumbled with the tissue box.

"Ja, wel. But certainly it is worth trying is what I am saying."

Boy oh boy oh boy, did she have that poor guy in her pocket! She looked up at Kees with affection and rewarded him with a bear hug – she being a comparatively small bear. I never realized Sally could be that manipulative. What had she pulled on me?

We explained Sally's proposal.

"But I think that is a very dangerous thing to do, Ms. Taylor. Is there nothing else that Dutch Intelligence could offer in exchange for information on the four killers?"

I'd been trying, unsuccessfully, to come up with something we knew, they did not know, and they would find valuable enough to barter for the identities and locations of four ex-agents. "I've come up dry. And I'm categorically opposed to using this information. A better way will come along."

It didn't. The days went by.

We leased a cottage that did look out onto the North Sea. Idyllic in normal times, it was set over 100 meters away from other houses, the lone structure of a housing development that had foundered, probably bled to death by opposition from local residents. We settled into Dutch domesticity as if born to it. The routine was comfortable. We rode our black sit-upright bicycles to the small *Albert Heijn* grocery every Tuesday, Thursday and Saturday. It was closed Sunday and Monday. On Thursday night we watched four American TV programs, beginning with *Star Trek*. On Friday night we often invited Dutch acquaintances for dinner, starting with cop Kees and his family. I prepared the meal, usually spaghetti, not out of concern for Sally's Delicate Condition, but for our guests' protection; she's not a very good cook. On Saturday we perused the fresh produce/flowers/licorice market that swung through our island once a week.

And every day we walked. That's what pregnant women are supposed to do, especially in Holland. Our options were three:

- Through the village. I was trying to memorize every nook, cranny, and hiding place should that knowledge ever be needed.

- Along the north shore until we arrived at the most scenic area. At that point the aggressive seals drove us inland. I especially favored the northern route as that took us past the little airfield where twenty to thirty small planes were tied down. Traffic was light; during the summer season there might be ten to fifteen arrivals and departures, most of them taking tourists on an expensive aerial tour of the islands. During the off-season I'd be lucky to witness any activity on the airfield.

- And along the south shore of the island where, if the tide were out, we'd be treated to a view of the mudflats. This may sound whiny, but a mudflat isn't much to look at.

Five weeks into this routine, Sally was starting to show. We met again with Kees.

"I've come up with no new ideas. Is there nothing that Dutch intelligence might be willing to barter?" I knew the answer. We weren't citizens and AIVD would hoard its intel capital for uses that advanced Holland's interest.

"Ja, wel. I think not. We must be able to think of something of use to Indian Intelligence. And do not believe that AIVD would try to fool the Indians – to tell them they had something of value and then give them nothing. The dealings among spies must not squander what little trust exists."

It all made sense, and that led us back to bartering knowledge of Sally's responsibility for Singh's death in exchange for four names and, if we were lucky, a path to the killers.

"We have to do it. I'm going to be waddling soon. Come on, Max. I'm making the call."

"Ja, wel. It is your decision to make, I understand. Now we must meet with the RID-er for our district, a man named Paul Detmer. He is based in Leeuwarden. I will arrange the meeting and tell him a few things so he is not surprised and refuses before he can think."

The widening gyre

Detmer did refuse. We met over coffee in Holwerd, the mainland port for the ferry to Ameland. "Kees, there is no way possible for me to become involved in such a scheme. These people are not citizens. You know my remit." Detmer had attended a training course in the UK and delighted in showing off his English-language skills. "It's limited to domestic intelligence, and, beyond that, I am not convinced AIVD would want to participate."

Detmer, another Frieslander, was also a towering presence and I spoke with some hesitation. "I've also been concerned about all of those things. We are foreign nationals who are threatened by other non-citizens. However, there may be no way to avoid unpleasantness. These men have been looking for us for almost two years. The mere fact that we're here talking to you increases our exposure and at some point it's likely that we'll have to confront them. Kees is rightly concerned about a shoot-out on Ameland, but he's also conscientious enough (I was hoping) not to ship us and our troubles to another jurisdiction. The relentlessness exhibited by these men persuades me it's going to happen. I would like to have some advantages on our side. One advantage would be to have names and photos with which the US police can initiate an extradition request."

Detmer's expression didn't change. I looked at Sally, who nodded. "Six weeks ago, as we were leaving the hotel in Utrecht the clerk informed me that an Indian-looking man had inquired about us."

"So?" asked Detmer. "People are forever trying to find other people to give them a bill, say hello, serve them with divorce papers."

"The clerk said she was instructed not to mention the inquiry to us. She did not, by the way, tell the Indian that I was registered there."

Kees looked offended. "Why did not you not tell me this at the start?"

We should have. Sally answered. "I apologize, Kees. We didn't know you. We were afraid that if we said we'd had a recent brush with these men, you would have had us moved into some kind of protective custody or something." Kees didn't look mollified.

I added, "We took precautions as we came to Ameland. We're sure we weren't followed. Had we been, they would've moved against us by now. As far as they know, we could have gone anywhere in the world. But they are persistent. They've surprised us three times with their ability to locate us"

Detmer's expression still hadn't changed. "Ja, wel, if what you say is true, then it can't hurt to ask. Perhaps it would be good to be more on the initiative. I have a meeting with AIVD in Zoetermeer Wednesday. I will report back to you on their reaction."

Thursday came and went, as did Friday and the weekend. On Tuesday Kees called to tell us we should meet him at the ferry terminal for a trip to Leeuwarden to talk with Detmer.

———

The RID-er's office was no better appointed than any other cop's in the Leeuwarden police station. I wondered if the whole RID network was eyewash to persuade the police and populous that the national intelligence apparatus was a benign extension of Dutch society, toiling in the service of the ordinary citizen, not a remote, uncontrolled and sinister bureaucracy.

Detmer offered us lukewarm coffee and reported on his discussions with AIVD. "Your proposal received a mixed response. True to their profession, the AIVD people wanted more information about you, which Kees provided." Sally and I looked at each other with alarm. "I don't know how all of it is relevant, but it's in their nature to collect information as instinctively as a squirrel collects acorns."

"The bottom line?"

"Ah, yes. Where did it all end? In the murky world of espionage one never knows whether one is shuffling toward an unseen cliff or strolling through a pleasant meadow. Zoetermeer will confer with their Delhi station. It is they who will have the final say."

On the ferry back to Ameland a defensive Kees sought to reassure us that the information given to AIVD would not increase our peril. Sally, who'd been teetering on the edge of a cliff herself that day, exploded, "So. You told them that two Americans, holed up in northeast Holland, wanted to know about four ex-RAW agents who had once worked in Bangladesh. Right?" Kees looked stricken. "And we're supposed to take comfort in the fact that our names were not used and the address of our cottage wasn't provided. Right? And, finally, we're to assume that no one will connect these dots. Right?"

"I will protect you Ms. Taylor. You have my word." Sally snorted and left us to stand at the rail, her fists white as she clutched the metal railing.

"Kees, she does have a point. Sorry she expressed it that way. We'll have to tighten our security or move somewhere else."

"I will protect you," Kees repeated with determination. His size was reassuring. The fact that he didn't carry a gun was not.

———

Sally did calm down. The emotional pendulum had swung back by the time we'd returned to our cottage. "I feel terrible that I spoke to him that way. He was only trying to do what he thought was best for us. I mean, we did ask him to use Holland's intelligence service. I should call and apologize."

She started for the phone but then veered into the bathroom. A minute later she came out, her face pale, her eyes frightened.

"I'm bleeding."

From Margaret Brown's notebook #1.

Medical care.
There were three components in Native-American medical care. The first was the healer (either a man or a woman) who was always on call and would prescribe the remedy and conduct rites of purification. The second, the remedy, were the herbs used; some of those are coming back into favor. The third was the rituals and ceremonies.
I think I'm most struck about the healer always being on call - and he or she actually came to the patient, not the other way around.
Try and get a doctor to come to your house on short notice today!

10

Surely some revelation is at hand

Fourteen minutes later Dr. Juffermans burst through the front door and pushed past in the direction he assumed was toward the bedroom. Over his shoulder, "Come please, Mr. Brown." On Sally's two prenatal visits Juffermans had wanted me in the room when he examined Sally, but those examinations had been external and the patient was fully clothed. Juffermans would ask while pressing lightly on her growing belly, "So. Does this hurt?"

I followed him into the bedroom where Sally lay on the bed, a small red stain on the sheets between her legs.

Lord, I know I've said and thought some unpleasant things about You in the past. Could we maybe patch things up and You could cut Sally a break? Not for me, Lord. For her.

With consummate gentleness, Juffermans explored Sally's nether regions. I don't know about you, but my reaction is that there's something disturbing about watching another man poke around in the vagina of one's lover, her legs spread, a glistening speculum exposing her hidden charms. No more blood, but an unsettling scene. Sally looked at me pleadingly. I wanted this to be a long pregnancy.

Meanwhile, Juffermans – I should note that he was about my age and ruggedly handsome – continued his exploration. I watched his face for signs of an emerging diagnosis. It was easier than watching what else was on display. He seemed to be conferring with himself as he continued the examination, now with a small penlight. Every few seconds he would murmur, as a mantra, "Ja. That is normal . . . Ja, that is normal." A few seconds later he would purse his lips and scowl. For every scowl there were two 'normals', encouraging the hope that the vote was tilting in Sally's favor. This went on for two minutes and I was starting to reflect that, in the larger scheme of things, Juffermans might also consider that death was normal. What was he finding that would explain this sudden hemorrhage?

In what turned out to be his final diagnostic act, he withdrew a worn wooden tube from his leather bag, a tube that was flared at both ends. He applied the larger flared end to Sally's abdomen and listened at the smaller flare. A few more lip purses as he moved the tube around, then a vigorous head nod of approval. He put the tube away and went to the sink to wash.

"Mr. Brown, if I may, a word with you," as he motioned toward the door. Can you guess Sally's reaction to being excluded from the conversation? If you can't, I've done a poor job conveying the essence of the woman's character.

"Oh no you don't, boys! Juffermans, I'm the patient here. Not needle prick!"

That was unkind, untrue and uncalled for. I've been in enough locker rooms to know where I stand in the rankings. Just above the median, if you exclude the black guys. Sally immediately looked embarrassed and sent me another pleading look. This time, I hoped, it was a request for forgiveness.

"Ja. Of course. That was not sensitive of me. Let us talk together." Head nods all around. "But, Mr. Brown, may I ask from you a small aperitif? I was preparing to sit with my wife and enjoy our evening drink when you called."

This request signaled either good or disastrous news:

- Option 1. Sally's problems were so insignificant that they shouldn't be allowed to come between this fine physician (I truly mean that. Fourteen minutes to make a house call? Match that anywhere else in the world.) and an ounce of alcohol.
- Option 2. No. I didn't want to think about option 2. It's clearly option 1.

"I have several different flavored genevers, Doctor."

"If it would be possible, do you have any of our native island *nobeltje*?" I did. It's Godawful stuff. *Nobeltje* translates, more or less literally, as 'not a lot of nobility.'

A minute later Dr. Juffermans was presented with a large snifter of *nobeltje*; Sally and I looked at him expectantly. He smiled at each of us in turn, and . . . went through an elaborate ritual of sniffing the foul liquor, swilling it around in the glass, sipping it delicately, then tossing down the remainder. I feared he would stand, shake our hands, and leave.

"And, your diagnosis, Doctor?"

"Ja. I have been delaying because I am thinking." He tried to extract another drop from his glass, so I refilled it. "It is not unusual at this time in the pregnancy for what we call spotting. The woman loses small amounts of blood. So, it is normal. But in the case of Ms. Taylor, this is more blood than spotting. When I do the examination, everything seems normal." He examined his glass which contained less liqueur than the first time. I splashed a few more drops into it. "I have an ultrasound machine in my office. I think to be more sure it would be wise to come tomorrow morning and we can look inside the uterus. Tonight you should not worry."

Juffermans sipped the remaining *nobeltje* more slowly, and took his leave, I, wringing his hand in gratitude at the door. Fourteen minutes!

———

The next morning we were waiting at the door when the clinic opened, as were several other people, most with medical conditions that took priority. It was almost an hour before the receptionist signaled us in.

"So. I hope you both had a good sleep. Ja?" We hadn't slept at all. "This machine is new. All the huisartsen are receiving ultrasound and because of my remote location this clinic is among the first. Please be patient while I learn. I received a few hours training in Leeuwarden and then they gave to me this machine."

Juffermans smeared some jelly on Sally's abdomen and worked a flat probe around while watching a small monitor. I had only a slant view of the monitor but would have been unable to interpret the flickering green and black images from any angle. Juffermans stopped, thought, and then began again. At length, he put down the probe and his assistant cleaned the jelly off Sally. We waited for a pronouncement. I was unable to speak, my mouth too dry to safely move my tongue.

"Well, it is confirmed." He stopped.

I'm going to kill the bastard if he doesn't get on with it. Fourteen minutes or not.

"Everything looks normal. However, you must take extra precautions, Ms. Taylor. You will continue with the exercise, but you must not travel and you must avoid any emotional stress." Fat luck with that. "Of course you must not anymore have intimate relations." What!? I intended to get a second opinion on that one. "The bleeding is a small warning. I want you to come every week now to the clinic for blood pressure monitoring. If you feel your blood pressure is going high, you must come immediately. I see you are healthy and so there is no risk if you are careful and follow instructions. You will have fine healthy children, Ms. Taylor."

"Thank you so much, Doctor. We just want to get through this one alright."

"Ja, wel, this one. That is the next thing I must tell you. Last night I think I heard two small heart beats. Today the ultrasound made confirmation. Congratulations."

From Margaret Brown's notebook #1.

Twins.

I had twin aunts and have always been interested in twins in mythology. They rarely occupy
the moral middle ground; the arrival of twins
is either auspicious or ominous.

My reading on twins among the indigenous
people of North America is incomplete, but
there is an interesting pattern. In the east
twins were either evil, or more commonly, they
represented the duality of the world they saw -
one twin was positive and the other negative.
When you get to our part of the country both of
the twins are usually positive. The twins Enum-
claw and Kapoonis tried to obtain fire and
rock for their people from the spirits. Their activities became so threatening that the sky god
sidelined them by making the twins into spirits
themselves.

My aunts? In our family one never speaks ill of
the departed. They could have been born
hellers and we would never hear of it now. One
thing is certain about twins, however: they're a
lot more work for mom and dad.

11

Surely the Second Coming is at hand

We walked back through the village to our cottage, Sally tight-lipped. At regular intervals she'd look at me accusingly. Her reaction to the news was evident. I was still working on mine. *Mighty Max – what a guy! – shoots his thunderbolts through damaged plumbing, navigating the perils of a hostile vaginal environment, homing in on not one, but* **TWO** *eggs!* Those were not Sally's thoughts.

Or maybe my reaction was: *Things are not twice as complicated as before, but somewhat more complicated. Twenty percent? Forty percent?*

What does Roscoe II add? A bigger and less mobile Sally? Harder to slip away in the night? Another set of vocal cords to reveal our location as we huddle under a viaduct while assassins with searchlights and German Shepherds comb the streets?

I didn't know I had such a rich imagination. Sally rescued me from further excursions into dark fantasies.

"It's not your fault." Off to our right a small storm was rushing across the grey sea toward the island. An omen? "Maybe it's a good thing. I mean, a complete family – all at once." We hadn't discussed family size for obvious reasons. But two children seemed to be the norm for the middle-class.

"I know, babe. We're well enough off so that tending two children isn't going to be an issue. I'm trying to think about – or maybe not think about – what this means for our more immediate problems, security."

———

Fatherhood. I was also thinking about that (as well as the 'no more intimate relations'). How do you learn to be a father? Forget books. For every How-to book that mentions fathering – in brief passing – there are hundreds on pregnancy and 'parenting' which, when you check the content, is all about what the primary caregiver/mother is supposed to do. There's really nothing for us prospective fathers, aside from humor books.

Did I have a great role model to emulate? No. As I said ear-lier, my sister's death had converted a pretty good father into a physical shell, an emotional void.

I went back through mom's notebooks – a cornucopia on euthanasia, suicide, pregnancy, and story-telling drawn from Native-American history and culture – and found them silent on fatherhood. Fathers were respected, but that's it. No guidance on how they won that respect. The most detailed item she'd written was about the father/chief of the Shoshones, Chief Poca-tello.

From Margaret Brown's notebook #5

Leadership
Chief Pocatello was inventive in his efforts to protect his people, the Shoshones,
but like all the chiefs, he failed.
When immigrants started arriving in the
Utah Territory he led harassing raids to
discourage them. Brigham Young attempted reconciliation, but the Army became involved and hostilities resumed.
Pocatello learned the Army intended to
'chastise' the Natives. He led his people
out of harm's way and avoided the Bear
River Massacre. Some chastisement!!
Chased by the Army he sued for peace
and agreed to move to the Fort Hall reservation in return for $5,000 in annual
supplies. These were rarely provided.
Faced with starvation he led his people to
a Mormon mission for conversion, expecting a sharing of resources. The mission-
aries eagerly baptized the Shoshones, but
the white settlers weren't in a sharing
mood. They called in the Army who drove
the Shoshone back onto the reservation.
When gold was discovered in Idaho he
bartered access to a railroad across the
reservation for resources. This helped
some, but all that really came out of it
was our city was named for the chief.

There you have it: Try aggressiveness; try conciliation; try integration; negotiate; cut deals; barter away your resources. The upshot? You're irrelevant, extended a meaningless honor, you have no lasting impact.

Irrelevant, without impact, given a meaningless honor? That's exactly what the humor writers tell us is in store for fathers.

———

That afternoon as Sally and I started our walk along the northern side of the island we were pleased to be joined by Kees who revealed himself to be an avid birder.

"Perhaps it is because I am a policeman, but I have always been interested in the plovers that nest here. There are several different plovers, but the ones I like the most are what I call, the 'great fakers of Ameland.' They often make me think of police work." The connection between police work and a specific species of bird required further explanation.

"These birds make their nests on the ground which is, of course, very vulnerable to predators such as cats and dogs. When a predator approaches, one of the birds – there is always a mother and father and they take turns on the nest – one of the birds runs away from the nest and pretends to be in distress. It drags its wings on the ground and moves slowly. The predator naturally chases the injured bird but as the predator gets close the bird miraculously recovers and takes flight."

"And the connection to police work?" Sally asked.

"It reminds me of insurance fraud."

I already knew about these birds. Their North American cousins are called killdeer and they'd nested around the runways on our Air Force base where the Flying Safety weenies fretted that the birds would bring down a plane.

To show you where my thoughts were, during this conversation I was applying the plover lessons to our escape plans. I would lure killers away from Sally by staggering away pathetically, and then . . . what? Jump on my bicycle, perhaps. The plan needed further work.

"Kees, it's so nice of you to join us. Is this by coincidence?"

He reddened. "Ja . . . wel." Silence.

Sally laughed and hooked her arm under his. "I'm happy for the protection. But the lesson in ornithology is even more valuable." Since the news of our existence, and maybe location, had been transmitted to Dutch Intelligence in Delhi she'd started carrying Roscoe (the gun) when we left the cottage.

"Ja, wel," again. "It is a small island. Juffermans told me of the news. Congratulations."

———

"A different side of Ameland's Finest." I was impressed by Kees' encyclopedic knowledge of birds. He'd described the habits of over a dozen species during our walk. "And I don't mind extra protection, even if he's unarmed."

"He's not. I thought I saw a different bulge in his jacket and I confirmed it when I took his arm."

"You minx!" Big grin. "He's packing?"

"That's what I said." She looked pleased with herself. "The cops in the Leeuwarden police station were toting Walther P5s and I wondered if Kees didn't just leave his gun in his desk drawer out of choice. A friendly cop on a tourist island."

The gun was reassuring, but it was also a reminder that we'd set forces in motion with no sense of where they'd lead.

From Margaret Brown's notebook #6

Courage in battle.
It was evidence of bravery for a man to go into
battle carrying no weapon that could harm at
a distance. It was more creditable to carry a
lance than a bow and arrows, a hatchet or war
club than a lance; and the bravest thing of all
was to go into a fight with nothing more than
a whip, or a long twig called a coup stick.
The world needs to fight all of its wars with
twigs. That's the equivalent of what our Max
had in Vietnam. Although it did change him.
Even though he never killed anyone he never
seemed at ease with himself after that.

12

In the 16th – 18th centuries the great European powers were going at it hammer and tongs in Asia. Often leading the pack in pursuit of spice, tea, etc. were our national hosts, the Dutch, who, with only rare lapses, comported themselves with fairness and honesty. Thanks to the dual advantages of superior arms and squabbling among the native rulers of the region, Holland carved out a large area of influence in India. It started to come undone in the 1740s when they sided with the weaker – but probably legitimate – faction in a power struggle in southwest India. Their adversary, Raja Marthanda Varma, relied on a clever mix of diplomacy, duplicity, and judicious choice of battlegrounds. I especially like the story that fishermen friendly to the Raja lined up along the shore, oars on their shoulders so they looked like a formidable host of soldiers carrying guns when viewed from the Dutch ships offshore. The same fishermen fashioned fake cannons. This helped herd the Dutch toward the Raja's preferred battleground. The result? The Dutch were the first European power to be bested in battle by an Asian ruler: the battle of Colachel.

A professional writer might label this historical tidbit foreshadowing. I call it revealing: the straight-forward and earnest Dutch outflanked by a clever rival who plays by different rules.

A vast image out of Spiritus Mundi troubles my sight

Kees joined us on schedule – as he had done for two weeks – as we prepared to depart the cottage for our maternal-health stroll.

"Today it is better we do not walk." The deep concern on his face was alarming.

"Of course, Kees, and the weather looks bad, but what's happened?"

"I am so ashamed." He did look ashamed. "Sally was right to be concerned. Detmer called to say that the Delhi office has bungled the negotiations for information about your pursuers."

"Bungled?"

"Ja. Detmer believes that AIVD met with the Indian agents – your RAW perhaps – and asked for the four names. RAW asked for more information on your place and time of contact so that they could identify the agents that might have been involved."

"A bad sign, Kees. From what the leader of the group, Singh, told me, only the six of them were operating in Dhaka for several years. RAW didn't need any more information to identify them."

"The AIVD man doing the request did not know this. Detmer believes your connection with Singh at Dhaka University was provided to RAW."

"Were we identified, Kees? Or our location?" asked Sally, her face a mask.

"I do not think so." The concern that clouded his features betrayed his lack of confidence in the statement. "They may, however, find access to Detmer's name as the agent who initiated the request."

"That would lead them to Friesland. Not as secure as before, but still it doesn't put us in the crosshairs. What did AIVD get from RAW?"

A van pulled up and two standard-issue large Frieslanders got out. Our conversation was put on hold.

Kees introduced the two men, whose names I missed. "I have spoken with the owner of this cottage." Kees explained. "The police have a small amount of money and the owner agreed to share the expense of making more secure your home. That is, if you agree."

Hard not to.

We persuaded Kees to join us on our walk, if for no better reason than to escape the racket made as heavy front and back doors were installed, the attachments on the wood shutters were replaced by hinges that could not be removed without special tools, and latches were placed on the shutters so they could be closed quickly and secured.

"I am sorry we do not have funds to provide stronger glass, but I see you often have open your windows, like a normal Amelander. I worry that your cottage is so isolated."

"I'm starting to as well, but, getting back to our discussion, what did AIVD get from RAW?"

The hesitation telegraphed the answer. "Ja, wel, they say the information on the four men is very old and difficult to find. They will look but it will take some time."

"Not to be an alarmist, Kees, but three things spring to mind: First, I'm pretty sure that the names of an agency's own spies – even those that have not worked for ten years – are always at hand. Second, they think that information about the four is too valuable to give away for whatever was offered. And that leads to the third point: it now seems more likely that there's still a connection between the four thugs and RAW. If that's so, the thugs may be able to call on RAW's resources, and that makes them a lot more dangerous."

Sally and Kees acknowledged the validity of these points, then Sally asked the question I'd been avoiding: "What did RAW get for nothing? Was my name put out there? That was the plan, after all?"

"I do not know and I do not think Detmer knows either. He did not say and I forgot to ask because I was so shocked that the plan had failed."

"Could you follow up on that for us? That's a big one for Max and me."

Mere anarchy is loosed upon the world

Kees reported back the following day that Detmer had not picked up his phone or returned his call. Same report the next day. On the third day Kees talked to the duty officer and was told that Detmer had gone on leave and would be back the following Monday.

Unable to do more, we tried to relax. We took our walks, read, and I thought a lot about Juffermans' prohibition on 'relations.' I'd met his wife and she was a fine healthy specimen, but she was no Sally. Perhaps the doctor was cutting me off out of jealousy.

If Sally and I went about it gently, with care, it might be even more exciting. I was waiting for the right moment to bring up the topic. She was still having bouts of morning sickness which, the label notwithstanding, plagued her at unpredictable times throughout the day.

On Monday Kees didn't show up for our walk so we took the route through town. At the newsstand the national papers were, as every other day, arranged in a rack from most popular at the top on down. There was unusual demand and several people quickly snatched up and paid for newspapers after they'd glanced at them. The headlines for *De Telegraaf* and *Algemeen Dagblad* were identical. That was also unusual.

Politieagent gemarteld en onthoofd

At the top of column one, Paul Detmer, in his dress uniform, smiled out at us. Readers were spared exposure to more recent pictures taken by the police.

Sally paled when I gave her my best guess at a translation, then confirmed it from the pocket dictionary: 'Policeman tortured and beheaded.'

"The poor man." Tears sprang to her eyes, then she recovered, "Oh my God, Max. We have to find Kees. What if they did the same to him?"

Once again she wins the award for most humane, most decent, finest, etc. member of the Taylor-Brown family. My concern? The bastards are closing in on Sally and me. Where to now?

"Right. Kees. Where is he? Let's go over to his station, but let's try to stay in a crowd as much as possible."

Surrounding ourselves with people wasn't easy. Of the island's small population, many were at work, the children were in school, the elderly and unemployed were napping, and of those out and about, most were on their bicycles and impossible to keep up with.

A small village goes deserted? Like a bad movie, suddenly we were the only ones on a twisting street. I thought I heard footsteps behind us but saw no one. Should I hurry Sally? Yes, Remember What's Important. Better a little blood leaking from the uterus than a lot geysering from the carotid artery. "Come on babe. Want me to carry you?"

"Me pregnant and you laid up with a bad back? Let's limit our losses, Hercules." And she started jogging.

We hadn't gone 20 meters before I heard the footsteps behind us again, this time distinct, and now also running. "Dr. Brown. Dr. Brown. Stop. I must talk with you."

Not a chance! We sped up. I looked back and saw a man in a jogging suit and baseball cap, 30 meters back and gaining. Distracted, I stumbled, hit the cobblestones, rolled and was immediately back on my feet, closing the short distance to Sally. "Sally," I hissed, "I'm going to do the plover. Keep moving." I wondered if she understood, then I stumbled again and sprawled on the street until I saw Sally disappear into an alley.

My pursuer was almost on me, "Dr. Brown. You must not run." He slowed as he neared. That was my signal for a plover-like miraculous recovery and I leapt to my feet . . . and discovered my knee was sore from the fall and uncooperative. I hobbled into the alley opposite the direction Sally had gone and tried to increase speed. I recognized this alley as I'd checked it earlier. It was a dead end.

From Margaret Brown's notebook #5

Tactics in battle
The three primary tactics were ambush,
stealth, and camouflage.

Ambush. The key was to draw the enemy into
the trap. Warriors would arise on every side
and a massacre would ensue.

Stealth and craftiness allowed more
members to participate. The older warriors
could creep into an unsuspecting camp and
steal horses, making pursuit difficult.

Camouflage took many forms. Covering the
body in an animal skin; applying paint to
blend into the surroundings; or simply
covering himself with a grey blanket if
among rocks.

But the most reliable strategy was to lure or
herd the victim into a situations from which
escape was impossible.

13

Somewhere in sands of the desert a shape . . . is moving its slow thighs

"Stop, Dr. Brown. Do not run more." With only a short few meters before I came to a wall, I stopped, but didn't turn.

There must be some way out of this place. To my right a curtain was slowly drawn across a window. *Thanks for helping.* A bicycle was propped against the wall. *Any chance of leaping on that and racing past my pursuer? No.*

"I have information about Mr. Detmer that is important to you." *No doubt.* "Mr. Van Warmerdam wants you to know this information."

"Freeze, asswipe!" Sally. Always the one to pull our chestnuts out of the fire. She kept saving our lives and my most heroic achievement to date had been to get her knocked up.

I turned. Our pursuer was a downy-cheeked Dutchman, about my height, his frightened eyes magnified by thick Coke bottle glasses. At Sally's command he extended his arms out to the side. Sally, Roscoe aimed steadily at the back of the perp's neck, reached under his jacket and carefully removed a pistol from its back holster.

"Max, this is a cop's pistol, a Walther P5."

"Ja, I am policeman. Geert Bomers. I work at night time as assistant to Constable Van Warmerdam. My papers are in my back pocket." Sally gingerly extracted the man's billfold and flipped it open. I could see the gleam off the badge.

"Embarrassing. Looks like we've nabbed our protector. According to this, Max, we have Surveillant Bomers in custody."

"I try to tell you. Constable Van Warmerdam was called to Leeuwarden for an emergency. When he was told about Paul Detmer he called and told me to warn you. He will come back on the ferry this afternoon but he insists that I am with you all the time."

Sally returned the man's wallet and gun. "Where would you like us to go Surveillant Bomers? And, apologies for our behavior. We just saw the news about poor Detmer and are quick to assume the worst."

We went to the police station where Bomers locked the three of us in and – with some ceremony – brewed *Douwe Egberts* coffee, Holland's own contribution to the expanding availability of really bad java. He told us Surveillant translated as Patrol Officer, a rank just one up from Trainee, and that he hoped to make Constable within three years. We engaged in a brief search for another topic of conversation, but gave that up; there was too much else on our minds.

From the window we could see the weather deteriorating to the north. Would the ferry attempt the trip? The wind had picked up and the temperature was already dropping in the police station.

An hour later a pounding on the door was followed by a shouted exchange in Dutch. Bomers undid the bolts and Kees burst in.

"I do not know what to say. Everything we have done is wrong. My friend is killed in a most terrible manner and there is no doubt that you are in serious danger. I only hope Paul did not tell them anything."

"Kees, I won't bullshit you. He told them everything they wanted to know. I can recall the boast of their leader when his goons were about to go to work on me, 'What you have I am confident my associates can extract at no cost to us.' Detmer talked. I'm sure he endured great pain bravely, but in the end . . . well, you know . . . Does Detmer have a family?"

"They are in shock. They all went on holiday to a beach town near Rotterdam. Paul disappeared three days ago. His body was not found until yesterday. The police did not release the information until this morning."

"Sally, that means the assassins have probably known about where we are for two or three days. I'm certain they'll try to move quickly before we disappear. Kees, we need to say goodbye."

"Yes, I am so sorry, but we do. Unfortunately, the storm is very severe. The ferry is not going back and I do not think a helicopter would try to make the trip. I will check."

A phone call later Kees shook his head, no. We were going to spend another night on Ameland.

"Where is it safe, I am wondering?"

"Our house, Max. Detmer knew which island we're on, but not our address. And the reinforced doors and shutters should make it one of the more secure places on the island." I was surprised she wanted to go 'home.' Pregnant women have nesting urges, I'd read, but our little cottage was filled with menace. Almost everyone knew two Americans lived there and they'd helpfully offer this information to anyone who asked.

"Really, Max. I'm bleeding again, and more than last time."

———

Dr. Juffermans was waiting at our door when we pulled up in Kees' small police car. Three pistols were out and lying in the laps of Sally, Kees and Bomers. I was mentally reviewing martial arts moves.

Juffermans conducted his examination of Sally with the same timidity and care as before. I was obliged to attend. After washing up he turned to us gravely. A lecture was coming.

"You must respect my advice. I have told you that Ms. Taylor must be very careful. And you must not have relations even if the temptation is very strong." He sure seemed worried about me jumping Sally's bones. It was definitely jealousy.

"Doctor, our lives are not that simple. We learned today that assassins are trying to kill us and may already be on the island." Juffermans blanched. "Sally did exert herself when we thought we were in danger. Now we'll have to move as soon as the weather improves."

"I cannot allow that." Allow? Ah, the arrogance of physicians the world over. "The situation is delicate. She is now at the end of the first trimester when miscarriages are especially common. She must rest for three weeks or more."

Rather than argue, I poured Juffermans his *nobeltje* and Bomers ushered him out the door as soon as minimal courtesy permitted. I hadn't forgotten the two house-calls. Fourteen minutes.

"So, Kees, let's review. Any indications the Indians have arrived on the island?"

Kees told Bomers to start calling the boarding houses to see if anyone had checked in during the last three days. Probably few, as the season was winding down.

Kees had talked with the ferry captain on the trip back from the mainland. The captain didn't recall seeing anyone unusual on recent trips. Mostly just Amelanders returning from work or shopping or family visits. A few off-season tourists, perhaps. No Indians, but he couldn't be sure. His job was to guide the ferry across the Wadden Sea.

"I understand how difficult it is now to see who is on the ferry. Today it was so cold that many had hoods up and I could not see the faces.

"Of course anyone can hire a small boat for the trip. There are often many boats in the Wadden Sea on weekend days and no one will notice if one boat lands on the island." It sounded like Kees had concluded that our Island Fastness was not secure and the assassins could easily be on the island.

"I think I see where you're going, Kees. It matches my own strong suspicion that the assassins are already here. They would almost have to be. They wouldn't want to let us slip away again. They saw the newspaper headlines and know that Detmer's body has been discovered and that we're alerted. I doubt they'd go to a contractor again. It increases their exposure since a contractor might blab, or be a cop. A contractor also takes time to hire, and they have the scent of fresh blood in their nostrils."

That image was the wrong one. Sally struggled out of bed and staggered into the bathroom. I started to follow her but she waved me away.

"The storm might work in their favor as it will keep people indoors and mask any noise they might make." A wave boomed against the distant seawall to underscore the point. "I'm paint-ing a pretty gloomy picture here.

"Exit routes. Let's run down the options: The ferry is tied up. Unless the captain can be persuaded . . ." Kees was shaking his head no.

"We might fly out. I don't think I told you Kees, but I was a pilot and sixteen years ago was flying small airplanes like those at the airport here. I could probably get airborne in this storm but . . . I haven't flown instruments in a long time, the airplane will be totally unfamiliar, and the storm has probably moved pretty far inland. Taking off in a small airplane tonight would just be doing the assassins' job for them. But, maybe an option if the weather improves.

"Walk across the mudflats?"

"No, Max. The storm will be pushing strong currents across the flats. The tide hardly matters in these conditions. The storm will not pass before tomorrow morning and the sea will not re-turn to normal for several hours after that. The next low tide when it might be safe to walk across will be at nine o'clock to-morrow night. A crossing in the dark, especially after a storm which will change the flats and leave new pools is very danger-ous."

"Alright. I'm over-thinking this. We get through the night and call for a chopper as soon as the storm eases."

Nods of agreement. Sally emerged from the bathroom, steadier, but looking embarrassed. She reclined on the sofa while I summarized the discussion and decision. "Okay," she said, "I'll take the first watch and then catch some sleep. I don't want another scolding from Juffermans."

Her announcement was received with small smiles. It hadn't occurred to me that Sally would do anything other than rest, but, she was the best shot in the group. I tried to relax. The house had been fortified. Bullets couldn't penetrate the doors or shut-ters. Bomers resumed calling boarding houses.

"Strange. The telephone is not anymore working."

"The storm brought down the wire?"

"No. After leaving the house, all the wiring is buried. It is the same all over Holland." We looked at each other apprehensively. Something was coming.

The explosion rocked the house. The bathroom door bulged inward, then collapsed back into the bathroom. There was enough light through the dust to see a three-foot hole where the bathroom window had been.

Three pistols were drawn and trained on the bathroom door. Kees had dropped to one knee; Sally, prone on the sofa, was sighting over its arm. Trying to find a role for myself, I stood rooted in the middle of the room. Providing a target for our adversaries? Now what?

To our left the second explosion detonated at the kitchen window, knocking me off my feet and showering the room with glass splinters.

Choking dust and smoke swirled through the room. Dazed, I got to my feet and looked for Sally. The sofa back had shielded her from the concussive blast and flying glass. I knelt over her; she was speaking but I couldn't hear. She pointed.

Bomers was crumpled in the corner, his face raw and bloody, his eyes saved by his comical glasses. Kees started to crawl across the floor to him, then turned, "Lights. Turn off all lights. They can see us as soon as the smoke and dust settle." I'm not sure we heard him; maybe we read his lips or anticipated the logic of his command.

This was something Sally and I were good at. She darted in one direction, pulling lamp cords out of their sockets, throwing wall switches; I went the other direction, doing the same. Within a few seconds the house was dark.

Kees turned on the two police flashlights but kept their light smothered until he'd placed them on the floor in the kitchen and bathroom doorways. The two gaping holes in our cottage were illuminated. Almost immediately the wood in the floor next to the flashlight facing the bathroom jumped and splinters flew as a bullet buried itself in the floorboards. Another bullet impacted a foot away from the second flashlight. This was followed by two more shots that were wide of the mark.

Bomers spoke to Kees in Dutch and the two exchanged a few words in hushed tones. Turning toward me, "Bomers tells me he is 'functional.' I was fortunate that I was facing away from the explosion and protected by my heavy coat and hood. What is your condition?"

I hadn't assessed my own injuries. Apparently I'd been shielded from much of the flying glass by Bomers. I fingered glass pieces in my scalp behind my left ear, and there seemed to be a cut in the ear. "I'm fine and so is Sally."

"We are all sitting geese," said Kees. "They can move about freely and shoot and they may have more explosives. We are trapped."

I weighed in. "I think the fact that they're trying to shoot out the flashlights means they want to rush the house. They don't intend for this to be a siege. We may have only a few minutes to come up with a strategy." We all recoiled in fright as a bright white light from outside flooded into the cottage. This was followed immediately by a great crash. Lightning. I thought I caught a glimpse of one of the thugs during the flash; he seemed to be motioning to someone else.

Night blindness to the rescue. "That may have been a break. They were exposed to the full flash and their vision is worse than ours. This is our chance to slip away."

"Ja, I agree. But they will be watching the doors. They are four. They can watch all sides."

"Plover tactics." I was willing to try it again. "I'll run toward the village which is the direction they expect. After I've gone a few meters I'll fire back to make sure they know which way to go after their quarry. Remember, I'm the guy they most want . . . if they recognize me. Then you three slip out and head the other direction."

Sally looked unconvinced. Of course. She was concerned for the welfare of her beloved.

"Max? You with a gun?"

Maybe partly it was concern for my welfare.

Bomers spoke for the first time. "He must take mine. I am still unsteady and my aim will not be good." He handed me the pistol and three clips of ammunition."

Sally reluctantly showed me how to take the gun off safety and chamber a round, how to eject a spent clip, and how to insert a fresh one. She made me practice. "Eight shots per clip. Keep count." The tone was that of the firing-range instructor she'd once been in the Army.

Another lightning flash, not as close as the previous one. One of the thugs was clearly illuminated approaching the bathroom window. I fired as the light dwindled but only hit the interior bathroom wall. "They're closing in. We've got to move now!"

"I agree," said Kees. He took charge. "Here is the plan. Unlock the side door since it faces the village. Sally and I will start shooting through the two holes in the walls. Covering fire, I think you call it. The spies will be initially surprised which will give you a few seconds head start. Then they will realize that we are trying to do something and will look around. Some of them will chase you, but maybe not all. If we are lucky, more lightning will let us see what they are doing."

Was I taking the coward's way out? Wasn't this the safest job, running away? The other three were left like 'sitting geese.'

I unlatched the side door and cracked it open slightly to make sure it wasn't stuck.

"Now," whispered Kees and he and Sally started to shoot methodically through the two holes in the walls. I pulled the door open and ran as quickly and as low as possible. The path from the door was paved with flagstones that were uneven and threatened to trip me. I hadn't gone ten meters when another lightning flash lit up the house and garden. A thug was crouched, aiming at the house, not five meters to my right. I fired two quick rounds as the flash faded. The thug spun like a top and pitched over onto the ground. Well, alright, Max! A lucky shot at the most opportune of all possible times.

My vision had been affected by the lightning so I had to slow down and pick up my feet in an exaggerated fashion as I continued across the garden. Shouts in what I assumed was Hindi could be heard on two sides, and then the unmistakable spit of a silencer. I fired toward both voices without slowing. Accuracy – if that were even within my reach – was not important. Luring these brutes away from Sally was.

More shots from silencers. No damage to me. They were firing as blindly as I was. I only hoped Sally, Kees, and Bomers were slipping away on the far side of the cottage.

I was getting close to the houses in the village, windows shedding soft yellow light in the driving rain. No plan had been discussed for the rest of the escape. Should I avoid the light and reduce the likelihood I'd be shot at? Or should I continue with the plover ploy, pulling my pursuers forward in their quest for a kill?

Plover. I veered toward the nearest house and as the light reached me I started an exaggerated limp, dragging my left leg along.

Here's a difference between plovers and humans: Plover predators don't pack guns. A bullet whirred past my head and crashed through the window of the house. There was a shout from inside and the front door flew open. "Get the fuck back inside," I shouted, as another bullet impacted the stucco wall. The door closed as quickly as it'd opened.

Plover, shmover. I took off at flank speed again. All that daily walking had been good for something. Back in relative darkness, I darted northward into an alley – not a dead end – and crept silently along, watching over my shoulder. It worked. Three assassins ran by the alley. Fifty meters further I was out of the village where I doubled back toward the cottage and Sally.

In our hasty planning we'd not assumed there'd be a successful outcome and that a rendezvous point would be needed. There was a small boathouse 400 meters west of our cottage. They were supposed to head to the west. Would they stop there? Maybe, if Bomers were in trouble.

I approached our cottage. It looked deserted. "Sally?" in a stage whisper that just carried above the hiss of the rain. Somewhere to my left the spit of a silencer was the answer. Presumably the guy I'd wounded. Down but not out of the action. Should I finish him off? *That's presumptuous. One lucky shot doesn't mean you're on a roll, Max. Remember What's Important.* I started to run again.

The terrain was more difficult. I couldn't find the little path we'd explored one sunny day weeks ago. The 'beach' was made up of large boulders. Difficult to navigate during daylight; impassable in the dark. Behind the seawall the grass grew high and grabbed at feet and legs. I slowed to a walk. Would the wounded thug figure out what was happening and try to summon the other three? Of course he would. In no more time than it took to remove the silencer from his gun he started firing rhythmically. No thunder to conceal the sound. The others would read this as a message.

I kept moving. My night vision was returning and I could make out the boathouse ahead. When I got to within 10 meters of it, I called out, "Sally and the Roscoes; it's me." I thought the mention of the Roscoes would identify me.

She wasn't the one I needed to convince. From close behind, "Put your hands in the air or I will shoot you."

From Margaret Brown's notebook #7.

Codes

Even though they were forced out of sight onto reservations, the Native Americans were prohibited from using their native languages. They were even punished if caught speaking in their native tongues.

Then, toward the end of WWI it occurred to someone that these languages might be used as codes. During WWII the idea really took hold and 200 Native American draftees from 33 tribes created a hybrid language that only they understood. They used it primarily in battle zones for radio communications. The Germans and Japanese never cracked it.

14

"Kees. You scared the shit out of me. It's me, Max." Kees had been standing sentry away from the hiding place. He was pretty good at his job. He lowered the gun and we went into the boat-house.

Sally was shivering in thin wet clothes. Her hasty departure from the cottage hadn't allowed time to dress for the occasion. Bomers was huddled against the wall; I wondered if he might go into shock.

We exchanged stories. Theirs was straight-forward. A light-ning flash revealed three thugs heading after me – they didn't know I'd winged one – so they slipped out and headed west. Bomers was having increasing difficulty walking so they holed up in the boathouse. Sally thought she might have nicked one of the thugs since he was holding his arm when last seen pursuing me. I couldn't confirm.

"Okay. Maybe one lightly injured, one more severely hurt since he didn't join in the chase. What will be their next move?"

The question was received with silence. Apparently I was now the group's tactician. I continued.

"Option 1. They think they know where to look for us, and they do need to finish this tonight. Our prospects improve with daylight. Theirs decline.

"Option 2. They have no idea where to resume the search. They have two wounded so they . . ."

"Mijn God! Juffermans. Maybe they will go to his clinic for medical supplies or, if they need attention, his home address is on the clinic door and only a few steps away." That's Kees, charged with protecting all the denizens of Ameland, not just the troublesome Americans that wander in.

We had our own reasons to find Juffermans. Whenever the now distant lightning illuminated the boathouse, Bomers' face was damp and white, his lips blue, and he seemed agitated. I recalled these as classic symptoms of someone going into shock. Sally was starting to shudder from the penetrating cold. How long until hypothermia?

"We have to move. We have two of our own that need attention. Kees, you steady Bomers. I'll lead and Sally, you bring up the rear." This didn't work because I had no idea where to find the path among the scrub trees. Kees, half carrying Bomers, moved to the lead and took us on a route well around our cottage back to the village.

"Wait here," said Kees. "The Indians have no reason to believe I am involved. I can walk more openly in the street. I will check Juffermans' clinic." One minute later he was back. "No sign of forced entry. Let us go. I have a key."

Staying in the shadows where possible, we crept toward the clinic. Kees had a key, but he had lots of keys. After much fumbling and experimentation, he pushed the door open and peered inside.

The warmth of the clinic was welcome. Sally found blankets to bundle up in, her back pressed against a radiator. Bomers was placed on a couch with pillows under his legs. Keep patient warm; elevate legs above heart. That exhausted my knowledge of treatment for shock.

Locating the phone on the receptionist's desk, I called Juffermans – I knew his number by heart – while the others watched. Bomers needed a competent medical professional, and Juffermans' was it, despite his crackpot ideas about sex and pregnancy. The first words from the phone were in Dutch and I regretted not asking Kees to make the call. "Dr. Juffermans, it's Max Brown. We have two people who need medical attention. Could you come over to your clinic?" There was a pause.

"No. Not now. It would not be convenient. Please come in the morning during regular hours." And he hung up.

"Fuckity, fuckity, fuck, fuck, fuck!" This infantile outburst was greeted with expressions of alarm. "The thugs have Juffermans. And they probably didn't miss the significance of our conversation being in English. With pistols to the heads of his wife and daughter, he'll tell them we're in the clinic. We've got to take cover." Sally pulled the blankets closer to her and extended Roscoe (the gun) out through the folds.

"The door is reinforced because of the drugs that are kept here." Kees paused, then added, "Only because it is national policy." Did he add that second sentence in defense of his island as a drug-free haven? Such precautions weren't needed, but imposed?

Focus Max.

"First let us put Bomers in the back where he is less exposed. He cannot contribute anything right now." Kees and I helped the young policeman to the one bed the clinic had in the back room.

We returned to Sally in the clinic's waiting room and Kees gave us his professional assessment. "I am thinking the Indians will believe we are weakened because we came here and so they will soon attack."

This statement was punctuated by a thud as a shoulder slammed into the clinic door.

Kees shouted at the door, "This is Constable Kees Van Warmerdam. You are under arrest. Place your weapons on the ground and your hands behind your head. Failure to comply will result in potentially fatal measures being taken against you."

I thought I heard laughter from the other side of the door.

"I am required to say that before I can discharge my weapon," he explained. He must have forgotten out at the cottage.

Sally was shuddering more violently. I didn't see her aiming a gun accurately. Bomers was out of it. And there was me, clenching the Walther P5 as if it were trying to escape my grip. Yes, we were weakened, and trapped.

What was on the second floor? I ran up the stairs and into the front room. Nothing but patient records and files. I edged through the dark room toward the window and looked down. Two men were studying the door and talking. Pretty relaxed. A perfect opportunity. I steadied Bomers' pistol on the window glass and aimed at the top of the head of the thug most directly beneath me. The usual thoughts about what a miserable shot I am flooded in. *Another lucky shot would be welcome, God.* Assuming God's okay with murdering assassins. The target was only ten feet away. How could anyone miss?

Here's how: Jerk the trigger, try to correct for that by simultaneously pulling the gun down, wince as the shot is fired, and shoot through a medium that might deflect the path of the bullet. The thug howled, fired two quick shots that took out the second story window, and hopped around, holding his foot.

Well, that was something, the foot.

Then both assassins disappeared in opposite directions. I was too discouraged to fire again and the opportunity was gone.

Kees ran into the room and I explained what had happened. "It appears that Sally was right. You are no good with a gun." *Could we leave this topic alone for a while?* Kees studied the street below. Hoping for inspiration? None came.

Back downstairs, Sally's color was improving. I noticed her clothes were draped over the radiator. My darling pregnant woman was naked under the blankets. She was still shivering, but not as heavily as before.

"I don't know that we can stay here," said Kees. "The doors are strong, but if these men have more explosives . . . and of course the windows are what you see." What we could see were two large frosted windows with embedded thin wire mesh for reinforcement. "I assume they have not tried to come through the windows because they think we will shoot them." Clever Sally had positioned herself so she had a good view of both windows.

I checked on Bomers in the backroom and noticed the rear door was oversized. "The backdoor looks larger than the front, Kees? Is that a vulnerability for us?"

"Yes, it is bigger. For the removing of bodies. This clinic has been here many years so it is inevitable that the 'failures' would occur and need to be removed. A more private way of taking away the bodies is desirable. That was agreed when, more than fifty years ago, a very fat man died during the night on the bed the clinic keeps. When the doctor checked on him in the morning the dead man was already becoming stiff and he may have started to swell because he would no longer fit through the front door on the stretcher. The story is that certain modifications had to be made to the body before all the pieces could be removed from the clinic and buried. The family was very upset. The Council approved funds for a larger back door."

Why were we talking about this? Escaping our current reality?

"There have been reports over the years of a very fat ghost in the clinic but I have never seen anything myself."

"Fascinating. Coming back to the present . . ."

"Of course. I refuse to think because I do not know what to do for Juffermans. He is with his wife and daughter."

"Alright, we have two problems. We're trapped in the clinic and the butchers are holding Juffermans and his family. I was thinking, maybe we're relatively safe in the clinic. The doors are strong and we can keep the two windows under surveillance. The Indians would be crazy to make a frontal attack. We can wait for dawn, call your friends on the mainland, and the island will be swarming with cops, all of them thinking about Paul Detmer." Kees nodded. I wondered why he hadn't called the mainland already. Not important. Reinforcements were grounded by the storm.

"That leaves Juffermans," said Kees.

"I have no ideas. Everything I know about hostage situations is from the movies. This doesn't seem to be playing out like a movie." Sally was starting to shiver more heavily again. She needed to be in a hot bath to start her body temperature back up.

"We wait." Kees' police training provided no more guidance than my movies. Four killers were holding three defenseless people and we were powerless.

I nestled close to Sally, trying to provide body heat. The radiator had gone cold, perhaps on a timer. Her shuddering increased. I tried to maintain a conversation but no topics seemed appropriate. I knew she shouldn't be allowed to go to sleep. Thirty minutes passed.

The phone rang. Kees picked it up and a conversation in Dutch followed.

"That was Juffermans. I do not know if I should believe him." This roused Sally. "He says the Indians have all gone and we should come to his house."

"That's suspicious. Why doesn't he come to the clinic?"

"I asked. He is afraid that we are now the hostages and he would be walking back into their hands."

"That's bullshit!" I exclaimed, then was shushed by Sally who had cocked an ear toward the back of the clinic. I'd donated part of my hearing in service to my country on noisy Air Force flight lines. I'd heard nothing unusual but Sally had.

"The back door. I heard the locks and I'm sure I heard a door opening."

Kees – impressive courage – ran into the backroom, pistol held at eye level.

"Sally, you cover the windows and I'll cover the door from the backroom."

Providence stayed my hand, preventing me from shooting Kees as he re-emerged. But then, I would have missed him anyway.

"The room is empty. Bomers is gone."

"Sally. Get under the desk." She was still naked beneath the blankets. "Kees and I'll investigate."

We edged into the back room, then peered out into the alley behind the clinic. "That way." Kees pointed his gun down the alley to the left. "See the light? Juffermans' back door is open."

Acting more like a TV cop every minute, I crouched as I ran to Juffermans' backdoor, pistol held in two hands, arms straight. Kneeling by the door, I waved Kees through. He looked at me questioningly. Why not him? This wasn't in my job description.

Kees shrugged and silently crept into the Juffermans' kitchen. I could hear low voices from the front rooms of the house. A minute later he returned.

"Bring Sally. The killers are gone. Bomers had at least the good sense to come here for help."

Sally was waiting at the rear door of the clinic, her damp clothes in one hand, Roscoe in the other. "The coast is clear, Babe. Let's get you somewhere warmer."

Juffermans' wife met us in the kitchen and led us to the bathroom where she'd already started drawing a hot bath. Sally eased into the steaming water. What a great body! No guilt at noticing and acknowledging such beauty, even in difficult moments.

She looked at me with an expression of despair. "Out, perv. This is a medical emergency we're dealing with here." Was she reading my mind or the leer on my face?

Juffermans' wife and daughter were huddled on the couch, the daughter sobbing. Mevrouw Juffermans explained, "We knew there was danger when they would not remove the scarves covering the lower half of their faces."

"That's the best sign you could hope for Mevrouw Juffermans. By hiding their faces they didn't have to kill you when they left."

Dr. Juffermans' head jerked up. He hadn't made that connection.

I went back to check on Sally after she'd been soaking for fifteen minutes. Recalling her statement dismissing me, I knocked on the door and waited for an invitation to enter. "What's happening out there?" The only parts of her that were above water were her head and her hand which held the Smith and Wesson .38.

"The Juffermans are unscathed, but terrified. The thugs kept their faces covered – fortunately for the good doctor and his family." Sally nodded relief and agreement. "Kees is still here. He's been vacillating between whether he should be combing the streets or guarding us. My feeling is that the question is now moot. The killers have had over half an hour to either get off the island or hole up somewhere. Since three of them are wounded and they gave up their hostages – one of them a doctor – I'm pretty sure they're trying to get to the mainland." The North Sea storm had weakened and was now a steady rain; the wind had subsided.

"And I feel better. Hand me a towel, would you?" She stepped out of the bath. As she dried herself I tried to keep my eyes off her. The growing round belly made her even more appealing. Her outer clothes were still damp so she sent me off to ask Mevrouw Juffermans for a loan of dry duds. I thought about that silly prohibition on 'relations.' That needed to be addressed soon.

From Margaret Brown's notebook #7

"Live to fight another day."
When it appeared that the tide of battle was turning against them, Native American war parties usually retreated. Because all men of fighting age went to war, the loss of even a small number of warriors could have serious effects on community welfare. Rather than lose many men who had families to provide for, war parties almost always retreated when faced with the potential for large numbers of casualties. Set battles were avoided, and the tactics were those of stealth, surprise, and maneuver. If the enemy was alerted, the war party withdrew and tried another time.

15

Reel shadows of the indignant desert birds

Morning brought, as forecast, swarms of uniformed police and Marines. First to arrive was a helicopter, out of which leapt twelve policemen in body armor, wielding military grade automatic rifles. Taped to the inside front of the chopper's bubble, an 8 x 11 glossy of Paul Detmer and his family: a smiling wife and two camera-shy daughters. They looked like twins. I wept openly when I saw it.

Every police and military vehicle we saw displayed a picture of Detmer, dug up from an archive or file somewhere. The odds had swung decisively against the four killers. No one in recent Dutch history had kicked an angrier or more determined hornets' nest.

By mid-afternoon every one of the island's 3,000-plus residents had been interviewed, every structure searched. A fisherman reported helping four men launch a small powerboat at about 4:00 AM. Two of the men seemed to suffer some kind of disability.

Juffermans was able to fill in the medical details. The ex-RAW thugs had been forced to make a strategic retreat. One of them had taken a bullet – mine – to the pelvis. He had to be carried when they left. Juffermans thought he might one day walk with a cane or crutch. A second one – also my score – had been shot through the right foot and the long-term prognosis was that he would walk unaided, but with a noticeable limp. A third – Sally's score – had been nicked in the elbow, as she thought, and a bone chip was blasted off. His prognosis was for reduced mobility of the left arm.

The round went to us, but not a knockout. How many rounds would there be in this bout?

———

Before the day was over we'd been interviewed by five different policemen and, lastly, by two unidentified but well-fed men in pinstriped suits. Tiring of the repetitive questions, as a condition of our cooperation I asked the pinstripers to come clean and identify themselves. This led to whispered consultations, and, ultimately, agreement.

"We represent the Foreign Affairs Ministry." The pinstripes should have tipped us off. "RID and AIVD have told us that the trail leads back to you. Perhaps you already know that you are at the center of a serious international incident." We didn't, but perhaps we could have figured it out.

"The Dutch Ambassador to Delhi has demanded an emergency meeting with the Indian Minister of Home Affairs. In light of what has occurred, the Netherlands expects full cooperation from India. You and Ms. Taylor may be able to provide further information that will lead to the apprehension of the people who killed officer Detmer and who may also have been involved in the incidents last night. Please do not neglect any detail, no matter how small you think it might be." He sat back and folded his arms atop his expansive midriff.

It all made sense but we were unprepared for the shift. Last night we were a bad shot and a pregnant woman hiding in terror. Today, at the epicenter of a rupture in international relations. We told them the full story, beginning in Dhaka in 1982 and ending in Juffermans' clinic.

I finished, "I'm so very sorry I've brought this to your country."

"No, Dr. Brown. It is we, the Dutch, who must apologize for not protecting you better." I didn't buy that. The protection had been pretty good: one cop and his myopic assistant against four skilled assassins. I said as much.

"Ja, I am sure Constable Van Warmerdam's efforts will be recognized."

Then the implications of the high-level meeting in Delhi registered. "I may assume, sir, that the Ambassador will ask RAW for the names of the four ex-agents, names that were not provided earlier?"

"Assumptions are always hazardous in international diplomacy, Dr. Brown. However, in this instance, it is a very high priority for the Netherlands to apprehend these vicious killers.

Nothing less than complete cooperation is expected. It appears that Indian Intelligence provided the killers with Officer Detmer's name and location. A full explanation and apology are expected."

Sally joined in. "As interested parties, will the identities of the killers be provided to Max and me?"

"I cannot speak officially to your question, Ma'am, but it would be unusual to divulge information obtained through high level diplomatic discussions. This is off the record, but it is my guess that the Indian government, as the price of their cooperation – and despite their weak moral position – will want publicity surrounding this incident to be carefully managed. The public will only receive that information that will aid in the search and capture of the assassins. You and Dr. Brown are the public."

Perhaps my face registered disgust; Sally's certainly did. The younger pinstriper sat forward in his chair. "I see you expect more of an explanation."

I really didn't; what we'd heard seemed standard fare for mush-mouthed diplo bureaucrats. Surprise; we were going to get an explanation anyway.

"This has been an attack on many levels. Most grievously, an attack on Officer Detmer and his family. And, of course, the terror to which you two were subjected. But our institutions are also under attack." His voice dopped a register, his unfocussed gaze had descended to the floor. No longer the pompous and aloof bureaucrat. "You see, we – in Holland – have, over many years, created a society that respects all human life. Perhaps revulsion at the Nazi occupation helped us choose this path. Sadly, today everything I heard and saw tells me that our protectors of public order are baying for vengeance. Pictures of Detmer's mutilated body have been circulated – unwisely – and those pictures have tapped a primal and dark impulse. Perhaps I should not tell you these things, but it has been our conceit in Holland that we are better than the savages who commit these atrocities. All that is in peril. This atrocity is an infection that is spreading. I do not wish to see us turn away from the enlightened principles that make Holland."

A subtle hand movement from his colleague. The diplo who'd been talking extracted a floral handkerchief from his breast pocket and dabbed at an apparently dry forehead. He didn't look as overwrought as he was trying to signal.

"I have said too much but you deserved an explanation." The sour expression on his colleague's face signaled agreement with the first part of that statement. "We cannot bury this story, but perhaps we can limit publication of names and photos that might lead to vigilante justice." He stuffed the handkerchief back into his pocket and glanced apprehensively at his older colleague.

The usual mumbled pleasantries and the interview was over.

———

Sally and I moved into the Van Warmerdam's guest bedroom for the night. We should have been too exhausted to sit upright, but after a light supper we sat in the drawing room, revisited the events of the previous night, and talked about the future. We gave Kees a rundown on the day's interviews.

"Ha! So, the Foreign Affairs man thinks you cannot know the names of the men who are trying to kill you? What world do those people live in?" He shook his head in mock bewilderment as he sipped his *nobeltje*.

"You saw our police today. You saw the pictures everywhere of Paul. The first policeman that learns the identities of the killers will want to tell you. Maybe it will be me." His voice rose steadily as he spoke; he was almost shouting.

"There is not one policeman in Holland who would not give you his pistol today to shoot those bastards." He banged the table and the cutlery jumped. Frustration vented, his shoulders dropped and, after a minute, he continued more quietly. "As you know, we are a somewhat pacifist society. We do not execute for any crime. But the pictures of Detmer after his death have been seen by most police. Not tell you the names? Those pictures . . . " Kees shook his head again, marveling at the naiveté of diplomats. The Foreign Affairs guy was right; the infection had taken hold.

Kees' wife put her hand on his arm and smiled consolingly. She knew what was coming next. The big policeman started to shake with grief. Fatigue and grief. "Paul . . . Paul . . . Paul . . ."

We sat in awkward silence as Kees released his anguish and despair. His wife wrapped her arms around him and drew his head to her. I was starting to feel dampness around my own eyes and saw that Sally was crying softly. But we knew this was Kees' time to mourn, not ours.

Kees brought his emotions back under control and, wiping his eyes with his sleeve, asked, "Is this how men become bad? I am a policeman, sworn to uphold the law. I should have no thoughts of execution. But I can see myself killing these men with satisfaction. That is not right but it is how I am right now." This admission triggered another brief breakdown.

What an interesting man, our friend, Kees. He cries at the death of a colleague and he cries at the prospect of avenging his colleague's death. Within the space of five minutes.

Kees rallied. "What for the future? Will you stay here for the delivery of the twins? Will you go somewhere and hide? Have you even been able to think about these things?"

I'd thought about them a lot but the day had been filled with interviews. "Sally and I haven't had a chance to discuss any of this. And right now, I don't know if my head is clear enough to treat those questions rationally."

"Ja, wel, of course. Meanwhile I think you will be safe." We probably would. An army of protectors surrounded Kees' house, including to our delighted amazement, an Armed Personnel Carrier, three jeeps with mounted machine guns, and a temporary command center – a trailer – 100 meters down the road. When the Dutch do these things, they go all in.

———

"We need a second opinion." We were lying in the VW's guest bed the next morning. Sally knew exactly what I was talking about. The erection pressed against her backside erased any doubt.

"Tell me about it! I'd read that some women experience an increase in libido when they're pregnant, but, yowsers! I want you to jump me 24 hours a day!"

This is too cruel, God. Here's the most beautiful and sexy pregnant woman in the world. And the horniest guy in the world. And we can't do it? *Waaaaaaaaaaaaaa!!* I didn't want a hand job or a hummer; I wanted to make love.

I looked at her hopefully. She shook her head. "Try to think about baseball, Max. Roscoe and Rosquette come first. But, here's some good news: despite the vigorous exercise of the night before last, no spotting." That was excellent news. Maybe we could forget about Juffermans' injunction.

I looked hopeful again. Head shake again. "And let's keep it that way, big boy." But she did turn toward me and snuggled, her scent filling my nostrils, her hair everywhere, her breasts pressed against my chest, her leg wrapped over mine. Within 30 seconds I'd started to pump Max seed all over her nightgown and the Van Warmerdams' guest sheets.

That's not relief. That's just embarrassing.

———

"Your cottage will be repaired this week." Dutch efficiency! We were having breakfast on the VWs' glassed-in patio. Ameland was at its very best – sun, the distant boom of the surf, gulls wheeling. "Do you think you will want to continue living there?" Sally and I still hadn't talked about what to do, but I was happy to have Kees part of any discussion.

"What can you tell us that would inform our decision, Kees?"

"I have been thinking. First, the action of our government. They will not keep this kind of protection for long. It is mostly for show to the residents of Ameland since I am hearing from my police friends that everyone thinks the RAW agents are too weakened to attack again so soon. So, all this protection will disappear, but not all at once.

"Then, I am thinking the government may suggest you move. They cannot force you, of course. This is Holland. But someone may approach you with a plan for relocation. It is my sense that at some level there is a feeling of responsibility. Dutch Intelligence made a mistake.

"And now we get to the four killers. I think we will know who they are very soon. Maybe today. Where will they go? Juffermans says the one you shot in the hip will need to see a doctor soon again. Juffermans did not say this in words, but I think maybe he did not give his kidnappers the best medical attention. Perhaps there will be infections. He said he has received an official police notice to watch for three Indian men with gunshot wounds. The location of the wounds is described. That means every doctor in Holland has received that notice. The bullets all passed through, but Juffermans says a doctor should be able to tell when a wound is caused by a bullet.

"Back to the question, where will they go? Anywhere in Europe, almost. As you have seen, a car does not even slow down as it passes from one country to another. The country that is different is England where a passport must be shown as you get off the ferry. I only mention England because of the large Indian populations there." Kees stopped at that point.

"Perhaps they will not come back?" Mevrouw Van Warmerdam entered the conversation. "Perhaps they will believe that you must move and they will not look again for you here? Or maybe they even understand now how difficult it is and they will give up?"

I had entertained the same thoughts. Three of the four had been wounded, one of them seriously; that should take the fight out of anyone. Against that optimistic scenario, there's RAW's fame for tenacity, regardless of the odds.

Sally smiled at our hostess who hadn't abandoned her hopeful expression. "That would be wonderful – that we've seen the last of those four. I'm tired of running and hiding. With babies on the way we need a normal life." She gave Mrs. VW a smile of feminine solidarity, signaling a level of mutual understanding that Kees and I were not privy to. "Maybe it's that nesting hormone kicking in," she continued, "but I'm attached to little Ameland and our home."

A first. To that point we'd called it our cottage or house, not our home. Our 'home' was an infrequently visited two-bedroom apartment in Montreux.

I was on board. The only friends we had in the world were here, Kees and his family, and we had an expanding circle of Amelander acquaintances who stopped and chatted with us in the street. For the first time in our relationship we had a social life. We'd just joined a group that played volleyball (poorly) on Wednesday night, I went to a bi-weekly antiquarian interest club, and Sally had signed up for a cooking class (hooray!) that occupied her two mornings a week. I no longer agonized about where I belonged in the world. I belonged with Sally and the two little rascals in her belly who were waiting to make their appearance. Where else would we go?

From Margaret Brown's notebook #4

Home

I think we - the immigrants to this continent - view the land claims of the indigenous people with faint disdain. They say the land is sacred to them and they have a special attachment to it. I'm sure many Whites believe the Native Americans say this only as an arguing point to try to get some land back. Or that it reflects a pagan set of beliefs that we, good Christians, can safely dismiss as ungodly.

How many of these same white people have a strong attachment to their own land? I bet a lot do. I love our little house where Ralph and I raised our babies. I love our neighbors - well, most of them - and our friends, and our church. It's where we belong. Is this so different from the longings of the Shoshones and others to live and raise their own families where everything is familiar and comforting?

Here is an old Native American proverb. "Treat the earth well: it was not given to you by your parents, it was loaned to you by your children. We do not inherit the Earth from our ancestors, we borrow it from our children."

That seems like such a nice thought.

16

Vexed to nightmare by a rocking cradle

"Guilt, Maxwell? You have certainly come to the right country. I think we should declare guilt as the Official National Emotional Disorder of the Netherlands." The speaker is the island's sole clinical psychologist, a middle-aged divorcée named Marta Meyer. "Our European neighbors like to say we are a nation of finger-pointers. Always wagging our finger indignantly at the misdeeds of others. Why?" She paused; did she expect an answer? "I will tell you. It is because it relieves our own anxieties that *we* are to blame for something."

Like many others I'd encountered in the helping professions, Dr. Meyer was constitutionally unsuited for her line of work. Our weekly sessions were an opportunity for her to talk, not listen. When I say weekly, a clarification: This was only the second meeting and it was uncertain how much longer I'd part with 150 guilders to hear her spout theories I was already familiar with from my days as a professional sociologist. And the irony! Back in my university teaching days I was in the forefront of those mocking the clinical psychologists on campus.

My in-going hope with Dr. Meyer was that she wouldn't unload doctrinaire dribble from Jung, Freud, Adler, etc. I hadn't considered there might be other problems with her therapeutic approach.

You interpret my presence on the couch (not literally on the couch; we sat in chairs) as a sign of desperation, right? Yes, I was concerned. And worn down by lack of sleep. Maybe if that jealous jerk, Dr. J, would lift the sex ban both Sally and I would sleep better. But then, consider Shakespeare. Sleep? Perchance to dream?

I'd had a couple of dreams about suicide – when I'd been able to sleep. Dreaming about suicide wasn't troubling, and that was troubling in itself. In the dream I felt liberated; my debts paid off.

The other dream was worse; I'd had it once: A burning building; Sally's screams rising above the crackle of flames and crash of collapsing timbers; Max watching, helpless. A dream that cast a long shadow over waking hours.

All very worrying.

Every few days another event would stir the festering guilt.

- Bomers came back to the island after two weeks of reconstructive surgery in Amsterdam, his face still scarred. His marriage prospects, never bright, were materially dimmed.
- I learned that, although it was still winter, future bookings were down on the island. News of the attack had been well publicized.
- Juffermans' daughter was in therapy, presumably to address the emotional residue of the kidnapping.
- I didn't want to hear about Detmer's widow and daughters. I thought about them at least once every hour.

"But Maxwell, enough about Holland. Let us talk about you. Did you always feel guilty, even as a child?"

I hadn't thought that far back. I was the merry prankster, blowing up the plumbing, putting Saran Wrap over toilet bowls, shaking itching powder into jockstraps. But I had to do it. My sissy name made me an object of ridicule; to avoid ostracism Smythie the Fourth needed to appear brash, defiant and fearless. If there was any guilt, it was buried deep. This took a minute to think through, by which time Dr. Meyer was off on another tangent, this time theorizing about guilt and exaggerated feelings of potency.

"You see, Maxwell, I have had many patients (but how long did any of them stay with you?) who felt guilty about things that they did not directly cause. My own husband – as an example – even blamed himself if his football team, Ajax, lost."

And how long did *he* stay with you?

She went on for several minutes in this vein and then swung back to her client.

"Now, let us review again the things you say you feel guilty for, and in a reasonable way, you must think whether you are responsible."

So, we started down the list:

- Sister Debbie wanted to be in the front seat and I let her. She sat up on her knees, went through the windshield when we crashed. Died. If I'd held out for the front seat . . .
- Countless victims of my childhood pranks were hurt, upset, embarrassed, incurred repair costs, and so on.
- Vietnam. A scary part of my brain. I try not to think about Vietnam. Things can go wrong unless Sally's with me, and even her presence is no guarantee.

"Dr. Meyer. We've done this before. You know the list. I know the drill. I reel off the things I worry about. Things that I set in motion that had painful consequences for others. You say – or rather imply – that it's arrogant on my part to think I'm omnipotent and these consequences were due to my actions. I respond that there are too many of them." Meyer didn't respond.

"Am I a god? That possibility never crossed my mind. If I have powers though, they certainly aren't powers for good. Three members of my family are dead and I set things in motion that led to those deaths." I hadn't told her how dad checked out.

To my thinking, it all added up as pretty conclusive evidence that if I'd become a god, it was on the model of Kali, the dark destroyer.

"I look at my cherished partner and I want to shriek, 'Run! Save yourself and our babies!'"

Dr. Meyer was writing. "I can only prescribe a limited number of mild drugs. But try this, it may help." She handed me a prescription. My fifty minutes were up.

––––––

"Where have you been? You look preoccupied?"

For the ten thousandth time, should I tell her what's going on in my head? She's Sally. I have to tell her. But what if she thinks less of me?

"Babe, I've been to see a shrink."

"Vietnam?"

"More than that. I think I'm bad news for you and the Roscoes."

"What? That sounds like someone who's getting ready to bail." Her face darkened. "Maxwell Smythe Brown the fucking fourth, if you're seeing another woman I will cut off your apparatus and shove it down your throat until you choke to death on it!" I think she was serious.

"Not as simple as another woman. And you know better. I've been pretty down on myself. It seems I can't move without someone getting hurt. Badly hurt."

Raised eyebrows.

"I mean, if we made love, two minutes later you'd miscarry. Everything I touch turns to shit."

"Some sort of a guilt complex? What does your Dutch Freud say?"

"She's worthless. It's Mevrouw Meyer, the talker. You've met her."

"What does she talk about?"

"When she briefly focuses on me? She says I have some sort of a God complex. That I think I'm so powerful that I influence remote events."

"Sounds spot on to me. Not that you actually influence remote events. If I thought you could we'd be at the casino right now."

"It's not funny to me, babe. When a person starts to feel they're somehow pulling along a train of misfortune in their wake, it leads to dark thoughts."

She understood what those dark thoughts were. "Oh, Max, Max." Arms around me. "You're the most wonderful person in the world." *No, I'm not.* "You've told me about your three friends in Vietnam. The VC killed them. The three men in Dhaka who were tortured to death? Entirely on the RAW thugs. And Detmer? There are a lot of people ahead of you in line on that one, starting with the simpleton who gave up Detmer's name to RAW for nothing." You'll notice she didn't mention my parents.

"I know, but . . "

"How many die every day on this planet?"

She stopped. A course change was imminent. "Wait, I have another idea. Impending fatherhood?" She stroked my arm as she asked to signal the question wasn't a challenge. It was a question.

"That's part of it. I don't know how to be a father. The same feeling many guys must have at this point. That's a simple worry, a normal worry. I like that worry. It makes me feel human. That's not the big one. The big one is that the number of people I can bring to grief increases by two. Two important people."

A long thoughtful silence. We were sitting on our bed. She took my hand.

"Max, make love to me right now."

"Huh?" That was unexpected.

"Is there something you don't understand about the concept, Studly?" Red eyebrows up. She was having fun with this. "Let's screw, a right righteous rogering, hide the salami, shag, bang, bump uglies." She paused. "Hump, two-backed beast, make whoopee, pound the pootie, schtupp me, boink . . . c'mon, Max, I'm running out."

"You're kidding. You know that's not a good idea."

"Well, it's *my* idea." She slid her hand into my pants and grabbed my balls. "Fuck me or these little jewels are coming off." She tugged hard on them for emphasis.

How weird is this next thing? I got an erection. She pulled off our pants. "Now you lie down and focus on my face because I know it's still okay. Keep your eyes off my belly." I did as told although apprehension was starting to get the upper hand. "Oh no you don't," and she stroked me back to full strength and slid onto me. Oh God. So good.

We came together, something I've always regarded as a positive sign. Then we cuddled in the afterglow – I chased every dark thought that tried to enter my head – and we fell asleep in each other's arms.

―――――

"Rise and shine, lover boy." That fabulous wide grin. "The twins are still roosting snugly inside this morning. No blood. No nothing."

"Really?" I felt great. "Then let's do it again."

"I have another appetite that needs attention. We missed supper last night." She bounced out of bed and across the room. The most perfect woman in the world. But I wondered if we'd dodged a bullet. I was still Max.

17

What rough beast

"Finally we have names. RAW has delayed as much as possible." Kees placed a sheet of paper on the table. "It says 'Sought for Murder.'"

S.I. Kapoor

Gezocht voor Moord

Dileep Patel

Dileep Mehta

Ashok Singha

"You're kidding! Three of these – maybe all of them – are of teenagers. These are bar mitzvah photos. No one would recognize any of the men I saw two years ago in Dhaka from these." I looked at the wanted poster again, incredulous. "And none of the guys I saw digging at Lalbagh Fort wore glasses. Plus, the Patel picture, if it's anyone, looks more like the man I killed in the warehouse in Bangladesh."

"The police agree with you that these are worthless. They aren't going to circulate this poster. They didn't even complete it. These could be anyone – innocent men perhaps. At the best, they're school pictures. The names? Maybe those are real, but the pictures were selected to make our job harder. The police think RAW is protecting the killers from capture."

"These thugs are still with RAW?"

"No. The theory is that RAW fears these men would make revelations if they are tried in a Dutch court. If that theory is true, the positive outcome would be that RAW will try to get to them first and silence them."

"Or give them asylum in India."

"Yes," agreed Kees, "or give them asylum in India."

"The Foreign Office must be going berserk."

"Of course, but they also realize that the Indian government may have the best intentions in the world, but not enough control over their spy agencies to force them to work for the national interest. It seems to be a common story in the world today.

"There was some positive news. AIVD says that the identity of Singh's killer was not discussed. *If* that is true – and my confidence in these people is not high – then you are still the primary target, not Sally."

I took the wanted poster from Kees and faxed it to Lt. Riley in Pocatello, with the caveat that the information was not considered reliable by the Dutch police.

There had been one small break in the case. A village doctor in Belgium recalled treating two foreign men with wounds, that, when he thought about it, were probably from bullets. The two patients said they'd been involved in an industrial accident and their employer had denied any responsibility and refused them access to the company's clinic. The doctor, who'd vacillated between socialism and communism all his life, found this plausible. His records showed he'd treated the foreign men two nights after the shoot-out on Ameland. The wounds were septic (good work, Juffermans) but he'd cleaned them up and put both men on antibiotics.

––––––––

Speaking of Juffermans, he grudgingly lifted his ban on 'relations,' while cautioning, "you must never do it more than one time a day and if there is any discomfort or excessive excitement for Ms. Taylor you must stop."

Lots of luck with that, Juffer-duffs. We needed to make up for lost time. But you know how these things work out. The raging libido that had troubled Sally during our period of forced abstinence ebbed back to normal – or below – as she was becoming self-conscious about her shape. A shape that I thought was fabulous.

A shape that demolishes social barriers. A pregnant woman is a minor celebrity in a small community. Our daily walks of two kilometers out and two back became a series of 40 to 50 walks of thirty meters each. Walk thirty meters, be greeted. Provide assurances that the pregnancy was going well. Repeat the due date. Aver that we were over the moon at the prospect of twins. Yes, natural childbirth was the intention. Yes, deliver at home. Breastfeeding? Of course! And so on. Very pleasant.

––––––––

"Max? Are we making a mistake?"

"Probably several. Any one particular mistake in mind?"

"Telling everyone the due date. That's going to be our period of maximum vulnerability."

The specter of the four missing killers colored every waking thought. They'd disappeared, but they're trained spooks so their disappearance wasn't unexpected. And they were recuperating;

Juffermans thought two to three months would be adequate time for the injured to heal; physical therapy would take longer. We knew they were patient men. They'd waited one year to put the plan to kill my parents into action. Why wouldn't they wait until Sally went into labor to make their next move?

Kees had been right about the transience of our protection. Within six weeks the island's defenses were back down to Kees and Geert Bomers. It was upsetting that two months after the attack Bomer's face still looked pretty bad, but Kees said the young man was corresponding with a woman he'd met while in reconstructive surgery in Amsterdam. What did *she* look like? Kees read my expression.

"She is a nurse in the clinic there. You were maybe thinking of a lady Frankenstein?" That made me feel better. I hadn't been the cause of any death or dismemberment for a while and one of my victims was making a normal life for himself.

Sally and I got busy decorating the nursery. The first decorations were bullet-resistant glass behind steel bars on all windows. The bars were held in place by a second reinforced concrete wall that was added to the existing one. The modifications made the cottage look squat, like it was retaining water. These comparisons come naturally when you're living with a pregnant woman. A security firm came over from Leeuwarden and installed sensors and cameras, and we were given a walkie-talkie that Kees monitored.

Satisfied that – short of a moat and alligators – we'd done about all we could, we rented a van and brought back two of everything from the infants' department in the IKEA store south of Amsterdam. We painted the nursery a cheerful yellow, hung cutesy curtains, installed mobiles over the cribs, plugged in the soft night lights, and still, at the end of it all, couldn't escape the sensation that it felt like a medieval fortress.

———

Lt. Riley faxed to tell us that the State Department was unwilling to issue a red notice for the four assassins. First, there was the question regarding the authenticity of the information. And second, the names provided were common ones; hundreds of thousands of Indian men bore those names. Many innocent men would be inconvenienced and the killers would not be deterred. We were still on our own.

———

Spring and Sally's final trimester arrived together. Spring, in the Dutch sense of temperatures rising into the low fifties Fahrenheit and visible sun two or three times a week. All over the island gardens were well advanced. Knowing we had to do the same, I hired someone to pull weeds and plant an array of annuals – although Sally liked to putter. The ferry resumed twice daily service and, as tourists returned to the island, we increased our vigilance. At Sally's insistence I visited an indoor shooting range in Leeuwarden for instruction. It was no use.

Sally and I adjusted our daily exercise regimen in order to monitor the arrival of the first ferry. It seemed logical to us – although we didn't submit that logic to critical scrutiny – that malefactors would want to get a jump on the day. An early start to see the sights and have time for reconnoitering before settling down to an evening of murder and mayhem.

The ferry landing was in the next village to the east, on pleasant days an easy bicycle ride to the port. Arriving, we'd take up our posts on the patio of the coffee house opposite the landing. From there we could scan the arriving passengers, sip coffee, and – you know where this is going, right? – we struck pay dirt.

It was a cold wet morning, just into our second week of ferry surveillance. The bicycle ride, although only five kilometers, had been miserable. A biting wind came off the North Sea, blowing a stinging mist into our faces no matter which way we turned. It was not a day you would greet with optimism, saying to yourself that all was right with the world. Not surprisingly, the ferry's passenger load was light.

Partially protected from the wind by a newsstand, Sally and I were watching the arrivals when I noticed a man with his hat pulled down and a severe limp, cautiously descending the gangplank. His face was obscured but he didn't wear gloves and the brown color of his hands, clutching the railing, contrasted with the pink, chapped hands of the northern Europeans disembarking with him.

"Wait here." I walked as quickly as possible without attracting attention. Bingo! The man with the severe limp was joined by another heavily coated person with a hood pulled over his head. Also a faltering step, and, again, hands the color of chocolate milk.

Where were the other two assassins? They were the able-bodied ones and the greater threat. Had they arrived already and set up a base camp? I looked back at Sally and patted my left chest – where a policeman would wear a badge – the agreed upon signal to get Kees. She nodded and slipped away. Was this a good idea, splitting up? Too late. We'd done it.

I fell in line, five-meters behind the two limpers who were moving slowly along Veerweg toward the center of the village. The wind carried back a snatch of conversation. Hindi or Bengali for sure. I checked the coats for bulges. No bulges, but the coats appeared too large for the men they concealed. What was under there? I knew I should just tail these two until Kees arrived. But, what if they made a sudden move? I had to be prepared to take action. I reviewed the few martial arts moves I could recall.

I was following too closely and too conspicuously; the severe limper glanced back. I wasn't able to see his face but it didn't matter. He wouldn't look like the photos Kees had received. I kneeled to retie a shoelace. That's what they do in movies when shadowing a suspect.

Alarmingly, the person with the minor limp was trying to wrestle something out of his pocket. A gun? I looked about wildly for a place to take cover. So many people around. I had to move away from others and draw the assassins away as well. Then, the klaxon siren on Kees' car. He skidded around the corner from Achterdijken onto Veerweg, lights flashing. The two seemed unfazed by the approach of the police car. I waved, pointed, and Kees screeched to a stop in front of the suspects.

He was out of the car so quickly they had no time to react – frozen in their tracks as the towering Dutch policeman confronted them.

There was an inaudible exchange before Kees turned my way. "Max, you should come over here."

Was that wise? Did Kees need assistance subduing the assassins?

No. He needed me to apologize to two elderly immigrants from Indonesia, one male, one female, who owned a small restaurant in The Hague and were enjoying an excursion to the Wadden islands on the one day of the week that the restaurant was closed. The 'gun' turned out to be a small guidebook.

After what seemed an appropriate amount of groveling, "Again, I'm so very sorry. Can I offer you lunch?"

The Indonesians received this invitation with unchanged expressions, but quickly and simultaneously shook their heads and hobbled off toward the center of the village.

Sally – I'm sure she'd been hanging back because she knew I'd fucked up – joined us. She didn't say a word.

From Margaret Brown's notebook # 2

Guilt by association.
"The only good injun is a dead injun." While it
was true that some Native Americans fought -
or fought back - like Geronimo in the Southwest, the more common situation was that warfare was forced on the natives to defend themselves.
Chief Joseph of the Nez Perce was careful not to
give the Army an excuse to attack, but three
members of the tribe attacked whites one night
and the end was fore-ordained. Joseph and
800 Nez Perce fought a rear guard action as
they tried to make it into Canada, but fell
short of their goal by only a few miles. Three
hot-heads brought them to ruin!
The assumption was always that someone who
looked like a Native American was up to no
good.

18

As Sally and I walked the northern coast route – ferry surveillance had been suspended – Patrol Officer Bomers overtook us
on his bicycle.

"Dr. Brown, Juffrouw Taylor. I am glad I can find you. I
want to give you an invitation." The young policeman was
beaming.

"We're flattered and would be pleased to accept, wouldn't
we, Max?" I nodded, hoping we hadn't just bought into something dreadful.

"There is one special activity you can do on this island. If
you are not otherwise occupied, my friend and I would like to
show you this on Thursday." Eager smile.

"We're certainly free on Thursday, Geert. What time?"

Bomers extracted a small booklet from his pocket and rifled
through it.

"Double checking. Yes. The best time is 10:30. If we can
come to your cottage at 10:10 to collect you?"

"Of course."

"And you will wear clothes that you do not mind if they get
dirty and wet. And boots . . . boots that will not come off your
feet easily."

———

We assumed the 'friend' was the woman Kees had mentioned,
and the special activity was a walk on the mudflats, an excursion we'd wanted to undertake since arrival.

Both assumptions were correct. At 9:55 on Thursday,
sounds of low talking and movement could be heard outside. I
opened the door and invited Geert and Marjolein in for a pre-
departure cup of coffee.

Marjolein had nurse written all over her. Taller than
Bomers, and definitely better looking than him in his current
condition, there was a severity about her that's difficult to describe if you haven't witnessed it. Think Nurse Mildred Ratched

in *Cuckoo's Nest*. Sally and I exchanged glances; we were happy for Geert. We'd thought he might spend his life a bachelor, and here he had a shot at his own iron maiden.

The mudflats are not flat. Gullies and trenches crisscross them and you're often knee – or waist – deep in turbid water. Geert solicitously checked on Sally every few minutes to the point where she was rolling her eyes after each inquiry. He was trying to gauge whether we should walk to the mainland or turn back at the halfway mark. I was hoping we could walk the entire route, thinking, as always, how this might figure in an escape plan. I'd read that, of the 11 kilometers, the final kilometer was the most taxing; your feet sank deeper into the ooze and I was interested in knowing how well we would cope with that.

Geert kept up a running commentary on the birds, seals, tales of drowning (he could leave that out of the patter), the easiest route, and the most treacherous route. I made a mental note of the last.

We did turn back at midpoint. The viscous mud pulls on your boots and you tire quickly.

Back on dry land, and rinsed off, we invited the couple to join us for *nobeltje*, but Geert insisted they not intrude. We guessed he had other plans for nurse Marjolein.

Returning to the cottage, we found a note under the door on police stationary. Kees wanted me to look at something at the police station. Just me, not Sally, who, after the exertions on the mudflats was happy to be excluded.

"I wonder if he got some new pictures of the Indians for me to look at. I saw them all at the fort in Dhaka, but from a distance. We were trying to stay out of sight in the taxi and they were at least 50 meters off. Of course, there was the guy who tried to take me off the airplane, I got a closer, but clouded, view of him."

"Clouded?"

"Yeah. I was watching the cabin door in the reflection in the little video screen in the seatback in front of me. I didn't turn around for a good look."

"Well, if that's what Kees' wants, I hope you can identify someone."

I kissed her and left, but not before she warned, "If you two party without me, Maxwell, you'll pay until the end of your days."

Kees and I had never communicated by note before, but I'd been out of touch all day. He'd probably checked our regular walking routes, then chose this method to contact us.

I rode my bicycle the kilometer to the police station, wondering what topic wouldn't include Sally, and found the door locked. Kees, apparently, was off on patrol somewhere, so I sat down and waited. And waited. A small plane passed overhead on its way to the island's airport. That was remarkable only because the unlighted airport should have already closed. Pilots, I reflected, are not great fans of rules.

It was growing dark; had Kees given up on my responding to his note? He may have slid it under the door shortly after we all headed out onto the mudflats. His house was less than a kilometer to the south, so I rode there and was received by the smiling policeman.

"Max, a pleasant surprise. Where is the lovely Ms. Taylor? Not feeling poorly, I hope?"

The realization was immediate. A swell of nausea and I slumped against the doorjamb. "Oh Jesus, no. They have Sally."

From Margaret Brown's Notebook #7

A shining city on a hill? Really?
I'm proud of my country but when I
read about the indigenous people I become ashamed. I had no idea we were
an inspiration for Hitler's atrocities.

Hitler's favorite childhood game was
cowboys and Indians. His favorite
author was Karl May who wrote more
than 70 books about a cowboy who always won out over the Native Americans
through willpower and bravery.

During the German attack on the USSR
Hitler ordered his officers to carry and
study May's books about fighting. He re-
ferred to the Russians as Redskins.

He often praised - to his inner circle -
the efficiency of America's extermina-
tion of the "red savages." He considered
deporting all the Jews to a large reservation near Lubin where they would
slowly die from starvation and disease.

19

The blood-dimmed tide is loosed

The door to our cottage was open. They'd tricked Sally into letting them in. There were signs of struggle. Some blood on the kitchen counter, some red hair on the arm of a chair. Sally wouldn't go down easily. I frantically searched for evidence of serious injury, but had no idea what I was looking for.

Kees pulled me out of the cottage and we ran to the nearest house where he was immediately on the phone. Out of the torrent of Dutch I heard Detmer's name. That would galvanize the police into action, but the assassins had a good head start. I'd been out of the cottage for over an hour. The tide had come in and the Wadden Sea could be crossed in a fast motorboat in 25 minutes. Assuming they went on foot to the southern coast where a landing would be easier, add another 20 minutes. That was the most optimistic scenario: only 45 minutes total from kidnapping to arrival on the mainland. I was mumbling this in a low voice, hoping Kees would find a flaw in the arithmetic. The kidnappers were gone and everything important in my life was gone with them.

"No, Max. You are in shock. I too am sick with grief and despair, but I am thinking more logically.

"First, it is a neap tide and the water change is not so much. Someone who knows well the channels could cross but only 30 minutes ago was it safe to cross without fouling a propeller." This wasn't much help since the kidnappers needed less than 30 minutes to make the crossing.

"Second, there is constant radar coverage of the Wadden Sea. Any movement of a boat will be noted. It is true that no one knew to watch for a specific boat, but we might learn of a crossing and where a boat landed. That is being checked now.

"Third . . ."

"No third, Kees. What if it was an airplane? I saw a small plane enter the landing pattern while I was waiting for you. It only seemed odd because the field is unlit. A landing at dusk is possible, but unusual. And illegal."

"How could they put the note under the door if they had not yet arrived by plane?"

"There're four of them. The plane could have flown out for the extraction when they had Sally. The nearest airport on the mainland is less than ten minutes away." We ran to Kees' car and headed to the airport.

————

As we drove onto the small airport we heard a motor cough to life. A single-engine Cessna was starting up midway down the tie-down area.

"That has to be them. No one else would start up on a closed airport."

Kees turned on his siren and lights and accelerated toward the plane which had started taxiing toward the takeoff end of the runway. We overtook the plane and slid to a stop in the wet grass in front of the turning prop, our headlights directed at the windscreen of the small plane. After a moment, Sally's frightened face was pushed forward, further illuminated by a flashlight. We could see the gun resting on her temple.

"Jesus Christ, Kees." *Sally, Sally, Sally.*

The flashlight moved to the face of one of the thugs who tapped his ear.

"What does that mean?"

"It usually means you need to do something with your radio. Can you switch frequencies on your police radio?"

"Of course. I can go to the aviation emergency frequency any time."

"Try 118.35. That's the airport tower's frequency." He looked surprised. "Old interests. I picked up an aeronautical chart and remember the frequency. These guys may not want to be on the emergency channel that everyone can monitor. And 118.35 is probably the frequency that was last used when the plane landed."

Kees fumbled with the police radio mounted on the dash of his car. "Okay, 118.35. And now?"

"Talk. See if they're on this frequency."

"Cessna 344 mike foxtrot, do you read?"

"Aircraft transmitting, identify yourself." The tower. I thought they'd gone home.

A low voice cut in. "We want an exchange. Professor Brown comes with us and the woman lives."

I quickly unbuckled my seat belt and started to get out of the car when Kees' strong hand stopped me. "It never works that way, Max. No one lives when the bad guys set the terms. You know their history. We can agree to the exchange, but not here where they simply shoot the three of us and take off. We need to get them to a place where we have the advantage."

"Do you have a plan?"

"No . . . yes. Do you think you can fly one of these airplanes?"

A question I'd often asked myself. Sixteen-years ago I'd putted around the sky in these little puddle jumpers. Then I graduated to the big leagues: supersonic fighters.

"You want us to tail these guys in a plane?"

"If we can. Which airplane would you want?"

"That Mooney back there. It's a lot faster than the Cessna so we can overtake them easily." Kees looked uncertain. "It's the red and white one that looks like the tail is on backwards."

Kees picked up his car phone and dialed. After a few seconds someone in the control tower answered. There was a brief argument – Kees quickly ran out of patience and started issuing orders – and then clicked off.

"He will bring the keys to the red and white plane. It will be unlocked when you get there. But we must not let them know that you are here. Our headlights are pointed at the plane so they have not seen us clearly. I want you to go out through the hatch at the back. Don't raise it too high. Then go to the airplane you want and prepare it for takeoff. I will try to manage the discussion so they do not leave for five minutes. But you must pick me up."

With contortions I was able to squirm over the seats and out through the hatch. Staying low I crept to the tree line and then dashed toward the Mooney. Someone was there unlocking the cabin door with the spare set of keys that airport managers ask airplane owners to provide.

I grabbed the ignition key and climbed in. "Do you know anything about this plane?" The tower controller's reply was a negative head shake.

I spotted the gear and flap levers. Everything was labeled in English, but the airspeed indicator was only marked for maximum structural speed; there was nothing on pattern speeds. "Do you know what speed these things fly on final approach?"

"Yes, that we must know to better sequence traffic. This plane flies final at 70 knots." The tower controller held a penlight on the instrument panel.

I knew that the noise of the Cessna would drown out the sound of the Mooney starting; I flipped on the master switch and turned the ignition. The prop turned but the engine didn't catch.

"I think you must first with fuel prime the cylinders," offered the controller.

Of course. There was a boost pump switch. I flipped that on, advanced the mixture and throttle, and tried again. After a few blades the engine sputtered to life. I quickly retarded the throttle to reduce noise. I wondered if the controller would join us. He closed the door and jumped to the ground.

At the end of the strip I watched Kees' car back up, clearing the path for the Cessna which wheeled around and taxied to the departure end. Then something unexpected, but helpful to our side: the plane stopped short of the runway. The pilot must have been hired by the kidnappers and he was following usual pre-take-off procedures; it appeared he was going through a run-up check. I gunned the throttle and shot down the taxiway – just below take off speed – to pick up Kees. As the Cessna turned on to the runway I brought the Mooney to a stop; a stationary plane, in a field full of parked airplanes, would seem unremarkable.

Kees opened the door and climbed in. "They believe you are not here. They will give us their demands by the telephone in my car."

"Demands? I thought they just wanted me?"

"I do not understand what is happening. The voice on the radio changes. The man who said he wanted only you and nothing more spoke. Then another man spoke and said there were demands."

At that moment the Cessna rolled by, rotated, and was airborne. I taxied directly out onto the grass runway and pushed the throttle forward.

"We are not at the end of the runway. Is there enough room to take off?"

"We'll find out." *Sally, Sally, Sally.*

There was plenty of runway. I retracted gear and flaps and we accelerated to 120 knots in a shallow climb. "That Cessna will only go about 100 knots. We should catch them soon. A left turn and we were over the Wadden Sea where we'd been hiking a few hours before. I couldn't think about it. Life had been simple and pleasant.

Kees spotted the Cessna above us, to our left. We climbed and settled in 100 meters behind the other plane. I wanted to get close to my woman, but . . .

Kees turned on the radio and dialed in the police emergency frequency and broadcast Mayday. There was an immediate response followed by a series of exchanges in Dutch. Detmer's name was mentioned several times.

"Wherever they go there will be a warm reception," said Kees grimly.

"Right now it looks like they're heading to Leeuwarden. And they don't want to be conspicuous. They're at 1500 feet which is the minimum altitude across the Wadden Sea. I think we're also flying in one of the two designated transit corridors." Kees relayed this information over the police radio. As long as we had Sally's plane in sight there was hope.

"You know, Max, the Dutch military is the best in the world at hostage situations. You read about how they rescued all those school children ten years ago?" I had. Moluccan separatists took 105 school children hostage in a little village about 90 kilometers south of us. Their captors released them after four days when the children came down with a mysterious disease; the symptoms were similar to cholera. It was later revealed that the food sent in had been laced with laxatives. The teachers were rescued after their captors had been kept awake for several more days to soften them up. The Dutch Marines sent their largest men in who screamed as they crashed through windows and doors. The stunned Moluccans dropped their weapons.

Good to focus on the possibility of positive outcomes. The Dutch were inventive and successful at rescuing hostages. Meanwhile the Cessna entered the Leeuwarden traffic pattern on a left downwind. *Sally is right there in front of you, Max.*

"They must think they've gotten away with it Kees. He's flying a normal pattern, landing at an active airport. Trying to be inconspicuous?"

Kees relayed this information on the radio.

Why would they assume they'd gotten away with anything? A policeman had seen them leave Ameland. Would they use Sally to keep the cops at a distance?

"Our people will stay out of sight. After the kidnappers have left the airplane there will be the best chance to free Sally. I am told there are already six expert marksmen on the field, four are near the regular tie-down area for this plane." We extended gear and full flaps to stay behind the Cessna.

"I am also told," Kees had made a decision, "that each man is carrying a picture of Paul Detmer with him. There has been no instruction to 'capture the kidnappers alive if possible.' I believe the police intend to execute these men tonight."

That's what I wanted. I was carrying a picture of my parents. Quick and clean. Head shots that would drop both of the kidnappers as soon as there was any separation from Sally. I also wanted to stay as close to her as we could without interfering with the rescue.

The Cessna turned final and we did the same. Now I was having trouble keeping our distance and started to fly S turns to maintain our 100 meters separation.

Kees relayed more information from the radio. "Our people don't want you to follow the other plane after landing. It would make the kidnappers suspicious. They understand your interest but they want this as uncomplicated as possible."

Understood. *I'm right here, Sally.*

The Cessna touched down and I focused on our own landing. Sixteen years? A pilot can lose his edge. Our stealthy pursuit would be blown if the kidnappers saw a fireball cartwheeling down the runway behind them. I chopped the power and we started to sink. I added power and we ballooned. Pulling off power gradually, we landed hard and fast and bounced back into the air. Gravity and low airspeed settled the issue and the plane landed firmly again – and finally. But the jockeying with the throttle had chewed up our separation and we were rapidly closing on the Cessna. I stepped hard on the brakes and slowed to the Cessna's speed; we were now only 20 meters back.

"The tower says this is a good distance. The Cessna will exit at the next taxiway but they will not see our plane because we will pass behind them as they leave the runway. You should continue to the following exit and turn off. Then stop and wait for instructions."

As the Cessna made its turn off the runway I tried to catch a glimpse of Sally but the tower was right. We were in the Cessna's blind spot.

Leeuwarden airport looked deserted. Were the police at the right field? We exited the runway and were told to shut down. I pulled forward among other parked airplanes and killed the engine.

"Can we get out of the plane, Kees?"

"I intend to. But we should try to look like airport workers."

What was going through Sally's mind? If her captors thought they were safe the implications for Sally were the opposite. I wished there was some way of letting her know that rescue was imminent.

The Cessna swung into its tie down space and the sound of the motor died. My heart was pounding so hard it seemed it could be audible across the ramp. After a very long minute the door on the pilot's side swung open, and a tall man – not Indian – extricated himself from the cabin. That was anticipated. We'd figured the pilot had been hired and probably didn't realize there was anything fishy until a struggling red-haired woman was wrestled on board.

On which side would Sally get out? I waited to hear the crack of two high-powered rifles and see two assassins drop. The pilot closed and locked the door, then slid chocks around the front wheel and attached tie-down straps to the wings. Nothing from the plane. The pilot walked away toward a gate to the parking lot. My eyes remained on the plane. What was going on? Are the assassins waiting to make sure the coast is clear? *Don't lose hope, Sally.*

I looked for the pilot again and he was gone. "Our men grabbed the pilot." Kees had read my thoughts. Immediately four police cars converged on the plane. Approaching cautiously from the rear, flashlights were played on the interior of the plane's cabin. "Come, let us see." And Kees started sprinting across the tarmac.

I overtook him and reached the plane as the cops opened the doors.

"Het vliegtuig is leeg."

"Leeg?" I asked.

"Empty."

20

The darkness drops again

"What? Where's Sally?" This couldn't be.

A policeman ran up. "The pilot has told us that the two foreign men and the woman got out of the plane just before take-off. He was instructed to fly back here. He was warned that if he made any alarm his family would suffer."

Kees and I looked at each other in stunned disbelief. The Ameland airport was only a few hundred meters from the beach on the northern side of the island. The kidnappers could walk there in five minutes, get in a boat, and be halfway back across the Wadden Sea by now.

I was not alone in pursuing this line of thought. There were shouts and radio calls. Police cars, their tires screeching and lights flashing, tore off. A large chopper that had been holding south of the Leeuwarden airport came rumbling across the field and headed north.

Kees reported, "Police and Navy vessels put out into the sea when I made the first call fifteen minutes ago, but yes, the kidnappers do have an advantage."

"Maybe." I was grasping for any shred of hope. "If they planned to get out of the plane all along then they would have their boat beached near the airport. But I don't think they did. I think they improvised when we caught up with them at the airstrip. That means the boat, if they still have access to one, may be on the south side of the island. I've made that walk and it takes at least fifteen minutes. They might just now be reaching their boat."

Kees patted his pockets. "Thank God. I have my car keys. Yes, they would have to walk or steal a car. That is difficult in Ameland. Everyone is always watching even if you do not realize it."

I ran back to our borrowed airplane. Kees clambered into the cabin behind me. We were agreed that we had to get back to the island, but neither of us had any idea what we'd do when we got there. The engine came reluctantly to life and as we fumbled to fasten seat belts and shoulder harnesses I wheeled back onto the runway and pushed the throttle forward. No time to chat with the tower.

As soon as we were airborne, Kees asked a question that had been troubling him. "Can you land this airplane on a dark airport?"

I hadn't focused on that. I just wanted to get closer to Sally. I'd walked past the airstrip many times. The yellow sand on the beach would show up at night. The runway was 400 meters south of and parallel to the beach. But there wasn't a lot of light in that part of the island. Every time I looked at the short grass strip, set among grass fields, I marveled that anyone could locate it from the air during daylight.

"Landing is easy. Finding a place to land at night is more interesting. But, trial and error always produces something. Buck up."

This breezy response didn't sit well with Kees and it showed in his expression so I continued, "We have a landing light. I'll make low passes until everything looks right." That, of course, was a lie. Pilots of all stripes minimize problems. I was going to paste the fucker on the ground if things looked even remotely possible. *Sally.*

Leaving the throttle at full power, the tach showed the RPM slightly above redline so I experimented with the propeller control and brought RPM down into the green. Airspeed increased to 170 knots, well into the yellow arc. "We'll be there in seven minutes."

Kees was on the radio again. "They request you not fly low over the sea, looking for a boat. Helicopters will be there soon." More on the radio. "The Ameland airport manager has been contacted and made aware that you will attempt to land"

Attempt?

We roared through the darkness. A glow in the sky to the east indicated where the moon was trying to shine through thin clouds. It produced no illumination and the sea beneath us was invisible. The lights in the villages on Ameland provided the only reference.

I really love to fly. I'd never taken Sally on a flight. Too late now? Focus on the task at hand, Max.

I was late in pulling the power back and had to swing out over the North Sea while speed dissipated. A slippery airplane, an admirable quality in other circumstances. The placard by the gear handle cautioned the pilot not to extend the landing gear above 110 KIAS but as soon as we reached that speed the gear came down and I lined up east of the airport, parallel to the beach and started descending at 500 feet per minute. There was a little buffeting, but the descent was steady. The altimeter read 400 feet, 200 feet. No runway. 150 feet. No runway. 100 feet. Where the fuck was the runway?

"Mijn God! Klimmen!" I saw the line of trees at the same instant as Kees and slammed the throttle forward. The engine coughed as it tried to digest the rush of fuel, but we cleared the trees. The scare left us both shaken.

"Sorry, Kees. Forgot about the landing light. We'd have seen the trees sooner."

Sorry, Sally. I'm wasting your time.

Circling back, we set up a second time. 70 KIAS, 500 fpm descent. Half flaps, for a slower touchdown, wherever that might occur. Landing light on, this time. The beach was just visible over the cowling on the right. Then, a welcome event: Some angel turned on the rotating beacon on the tower. The tower was about 500 meters from the airstrip, so it didn't help us line up with the runway, but it was directly south of the end of the runway which provided a reference for the threshold.

With the advantage of this new information I saw we were high. I extended full flaps and turned the trim wheel to reduce the pressure needed to hold the yoke. Now we were low, so I added power. That looked about right, but where was the runway? 300 feet. 200 feet. 100 feet. I eased in power to slow our descent. *Where the fuck is the grass runway?*

We passed the tower on the left which meant we were beyond the touchdown point and still at 50 feet. The runway was only 800 meters in length so a long, hot touchdown would turn into an accident within a few seconds. *Sally can't wait. We must be there.* I chopped the power and held the nose steady. Speed bled to 60 and the stall warning horn began to protest. "That's normal," I shouted. Still nothing but darkness. Breaking the glide better than in Leeuwarden, I rounded out as the landing light illuminated . . . tall marsh grass? A pasture? A runway?

Tall marsh grass. We touched down. The propeller churned through the tall grass which battered against the leading edge of the wings. *I hope the ground is dry and hard.* With a convulsive chug, the engine stalled from the grass snarled around the prop and the plane stopped, the landing gear enmeshed in grass. I never touched the brakes. "It's over, Kees. We lived." Dimly visible fifty feet to our right was the runway.

Kees came to life and was out of the airplane, sprinting in the direction of his car. When I caught up he was examining the doorlock and ignition. "This is not good. The kidnappers tried to use a screwdriver or some such tool to open the car and start it. The ignition is ruined. It won't accept any longer the key." He demonstrated the futility of operating the car with the key.

"Kees, this is great news." The policeman didn't share my elation as he sadly contemplated his damaged car. "This means the kidnappers did *not* have a boat on this side of the island. They wanted the car in order to travel a distance that they didn't want to walk, probably to the southern shore."

Kees brightened at this explanation. His police radio worked independently of the ignition switch and he relayed the information to the choppers out over the Wadden Sea.

"Within five minutes two helicopters will be scanning the southern shore and the water. The patrol boats will arrive in ten minutes and join the search. We left here less than thirty minutes ago."

I calculated the kidnappers might have a maximum of ten minutes since they reached the southern shore. If that was correct, they'd still be close to the shore. It seemed almost impossible they would have had enough time to reach the mainland.

Energized by this turn of fortune, we looked for our own transportation. There was a Bicycle-for-Hire facility at the airport. We each grabbed a bike and headed south along the Strandweg, pedaling furiously. *Sally, Sally, Sally.*

When we arrived at the southern shore of the island, we were greeted by the movement of flashlight beams playing along the sand and water. Bomers had organized a search party. Perhaps 50 of my neighbors were fanned out along the shore and more were arriving.

A cry went up to the west of us, "Een boot." Even a linguistically challenged doofus like myself understood that. We ran toward the voice.

A motorboat had been pulled up on the sand. The man who found it was examining the motor and explaining something to Bomers.

"How interesting," relayed Bomers. "It seems someone pulled the fuel lines out of both the tank and motor and it is very difficult to reconnect them in the dark."

Sally never stops fighting. My girl! Pride was quickly followed by fear. She would have been punished.

Kees' reaction was immediate. "They're still on the island! Geert, call on the emergency frequency with your walkie-talkie. We need to direct all of the search here."

One of the choppers searching the Wadden Sea picked up the call and relayed the information. As during the previous attack, Dutch police and military would soon flood onto the island. Would that help Sally? God, how I despised my pursuit of treasure in Dhaka that had brought all this down on my family and my love.

Kees and Geert organized the growing number of volunteers. The basic task was to make sure every motorboat was accounted for. I asked to say something to the searchers before they fanned out along the shore.

"Dearest friends, I am deeply touched that you are here helping bring Juffrouw Taylor back to safety. I have to warn you that the men who have her are vicious and inhumane. You all know what they did to Paul Detmer." Nods of acknowledgement. "I first ran into them in Bangladesh where they beheaded two men and tortured a young man to death by stripping off his skin." That produced a wave of murmuring. "Please, please, do not take chances. Police and Marines will be here within an hour or two. Our job is to determine whether these killers are still on the island, not catch them. No heroics."

I thought some of the enthusiasm went out of the searchers, but it was the right thing to do. These savages would kill any-one – without a thought – who stumbled onto them.

"You know what happens next, Max?" I didn't.

"Negotiation."

"Spell it out."

"I am not an expert, but my understanding is that we have gone from a kidnapping to a hostage situation. Or we will very soon. They cannot walk across the mudflats before the middle of the morning. If they start now the tide will take them." Kees does understand he's talking about someone important to me who would be in that group of walkers?

"A row boat? It is too far. We will find them struggling on the water when the sun rises. A sailboat? As you know, the wind is less at night. And a sailboat is easy to see. If they cannot get a motorboat they must hide. On a small flat island where every structure is in use they will be quickly discovered."

This was growing pedantic.

"Okay, Kees. Negotiation. Let's get ready for that. Remem-ber back at the airport they said they would contact us on your police telephone with their demands? We need to have constant access to that phone."

"I forgot. The telephone. On the way back to the airport we can pass through Bollum where the locksmith lives. I think he will leave his beloved television for this."

Back on our bicycles we rode into Bollum, one of the three hamlets on the island. Kees roused the locksmith, a sour looking middle-aged man misnamed De Jong – The Young. The lock-smith turned his disapproving expression toward me several times as Kees explained the situation. I exploded, "You asshole! Four assassins have kidnapped my pregnant woman and you need to be persuaded?"

"Steady, Max. What I am describing is the car and ignition so Mr. De Jong can bring the correct tools."

"Sorry. But we do need to hurry."

De Jong said nothing and retreated into his house. A minute later a small van crept out of the alley and the locksmith signaled us in. He could have driven faster, but given the short distances on Ameland we arrived at the airfield within a few minutes.

The locksmith examined the ignition and asked, "So. What is you want? Repair or to start the car?"

"Start the car," answered Kees and I with one voice.

De Jong shrugged and inserted a very large screwdriver into the ignition switch, twisted it clockwise with a grunt, and the police car started.

Kees shook his head. "It is good the kidnappers did not have a bigger tool or my car would be gone."

I nodded. De Jong shrugged.

"Please return the screwdriver when you are finished." He looked at me, "I will pray for Juffrouw Taylor and her safe return." And he drove off, leaving me feeling deeply ashamed for my outburst.

We drove back to the southern shore to check progress. No boat was missing . . . yet. The further the search moved from the kidnappers' abandoned boat, the more confident we became that they hadn't found another motorboat they could take. Despite the isolation of their community, Amelanders didn't leave valuables unsecured. The reason, they were quick to explain, was the influx of immigrants from the Dutch Indies – East and West – into Holland.

The search was joined by increasing numbers of Marines and police as helicopters shuttled from the mainland. Again, Paul Detmer's picture was displayed in the choppers and on helmets. These guys remained very serious about this.

I fought off recurring bouts of nausea and despair as I thought about Sally.

"It is little comfort, Max, but she is the only bargaining chip they have. She is safer now than at any time since they took her."

I would believe that when the phone rang and I heard her voice. The phone was silent.

———

"Max, may I present Inspector Van Dijk. He is now responsible for this operation." I was uneasy about Kees being demoted. He knew the island, he was competent, and he would make every effort to save Sally.

"Dr. Brown, I am very sorry for this situation. You will be reassured to know that Paul Detmer was my closest friend. His torturers," Van Dijk's face contorted, "will be brought to justice."

This wasn't right. "Inspector, I understand your motivation. I hope we agree that the highest priority is to save the life of the woman they have kidnapped. Not seek revenge."

Van Dijk looked startled. That wasn't what he had in mind at all. He had to recognize that I was right, but the deep emotions fueled by the pictures of the mutilated body of Detmer were hard to overcome. "Of course. We must save Juffrouw Taylor," he said mechanically. A constable brought him maps of the island, presumably to identify areas that hadn't been searched.

"Kees, I think Sally's situation just got worse."

"How can you say that? Look at all the manpower. And they will stop at nothing."

"Exactly. They'll stop at nothing to avenge Detmer's murder. Sally will just be something in the way."

Kees thought about this. "I do not completely agree, but I see the danger. They are so focused on killing or capturing – no most of them want killing – that they will not be careful about the hostage."

"We have to get control over this situation."

Kees' phone rang.

21

Kees let the phone ring three times, then picked it up gingerly, "Hallo. U spreekt met Kees Van Warmerdam." After a second he handed the phone to me.

"Maxsh? Oh God, Maxsh." Her voice was thick and the words were slurred. "They're only letting me talk to you as 'proof of life', POL or LOP they call it."

A voice in the background said 'enough' and there were sounds of fumbling with the phone.

"Dr. Brown? I believe we have something you want. You have something we want."

"Yes, we'll make the exchange. Me for the woman, but only if she's unharmed. As you may have guessed, there are many skilled police and Marines on this island, all looking for a chance to avenge the death of the man you tortured and killed."

"We had assumed as much. That is why it will require all of your skill and discretion to protect what is important to you. What we want are three things: First, of course, is the money from the jewels you stole from Bangladesh. We are thinking five million dollars. Second, we need transportation to a safe location. That will require some thought on both our parts. And third, we will exchange the woman for you. Your presence is needed as a hostage while we make our escape. As soon as we have arrived at a secure location, you will be released."

Right. Released in what condition?

"Keep them talking, Max. I will bring Inspector Van Dijk." I frantically signaled no. Van Dijk's priorities were dangerously wrong.

Trying to be calm, "Your first point, the Fort Lalbagh treasure. The amount the treasure brought is 3.2 million dollars which is approximately the amount I still have today. It always takes a little time to get access to the money."

"I said five million. We are not haggling in the bazaar, Dr. Brown. Unless, of course, you think your woman and baby are not worth so much."

"The issue is access. If I have to raise additional money there will be delays and there will be no way to keep the police out of this." My hand was shaking so badly the phone was bumping into my lip as I spoke.

"I understand your point. However, you should start thinking about how to obtain five million without official interference.

"Let us talk about the second point, extraction. We learned tonight that you are a pilot. This might become useful and it may reduce the number of people involved. During the moments you are not thinking about how to obtain five million, you should think about getting a plane that will carry six people a minimum distance of four hundred miles without refueling.

"And in the moments you are not thinking about those two things, you may think about what we are doing to your pretty lady."

"Why you filthy bastard! Maybe I should let the police and Marines go after you!"

"That would be unwise, Dr. Brown. We'll be in touch."

The phone went dead. I was shaking and nauseous.

"You handled that well, Max. You did not let him hear fear in your voice. Perhaps he will respect you more in future negotiations. What do they want?"

"The obvious: a way out of here. They think I'll fly them to safety and asked for a six-place plane."

"Six-place? Who is the sixth person?" We realized simultaneously that Sally would be along for the ride to control me. She would never be released alive. "Anything more about the plane?"

"Minimum range of four hundred miles. Where would that take us?"

Kees thought about this. "My first guess is East Germany. The communist control system is coming apart, but these ex-spies may have contacts in Stasi who will protect them – for a price."

"That's the second thing. They're demanding five million dollars. I don't have that and no idea how to get it. You heard me tell the thug that to raise more then the 3.2 million I would have to involve the police."

"I am not sure that is such a bad idea, Max. Yes, I agree, the police and Marines don't want these men to live one more minute. I understand your reasoning: If we let them take over the operation there is a danger to Sally. And even if Van Dijk sees reason, there are still several hundred men out there with guns who may privately disagree. But, still, these men are professionals." He chewed on his upper lip, then continued, "I wish we had information that would allow us more control over events?"

"I know where they're hiding."

Kees looked stunned. "You do?"

"They're in our house."

"How . . ."

"Sally told me. She said 'proof of life' and gave two acronyms, POL – which I believe is commonly used – and LOP which is a small private joke. Juffermans throws around medical terms we don't understand and one of them is LOP for Left Occipito Posterior to designate the location of a fetus. We started identifying any location – mostly around our house – as LOP or ROP."

"It makes sense, Max. Your cottage is the best fortified building on the island. The kidnappers don't have to worry about a sniper bullet coming through a window or a surprise rush of Marines through the doors. They saw how well fortified the house is when they kidnapped Sally. What do we do with this information?"

"For the moment I think we should sit on it."

"Okay. I agree to 'sit on it' for a while. But two things may happen. One, the police are checking houses. Eventually they will get to yours unless we prevent it. Two, you do need to think about getting more money. These men will have to buy protection wherever they go. For that I have an idea, if you approve." Kees looked at me expectantly.

He was waiting for pre-approval? "That depends on the idea."

"I said before that Dutch Intelligence made a serious mistake and may feel responsibility. Generally they are good at keeping secrets. If I can contact the right person we may find access to the 1.8 million."

"Okay. I'll get to work on obtaining my own money. There was no mention how we would deliver it.

"Oh, and Kees, would you see about the plane. I'd like one that has a turbocharger. I think the Piper Lance has six seats and a range of almost 1,000 miles, but there are others. I'd rather not borrow another plane and wreck it like the last one."

Kees made two brief phone calls. His expression indicated he wasn't making progress. "We must check together at the airport. I think 'borrowing' is what you will have to do. It appears there are many levels of bureaucracy to obtain a plane from the military or police. From what I have just been told, if we try to rent a plane they will demand to see your license, take you for a check-ride, inspect your medical certificate, and so on. I know how complex these things are."

He was right. There was no way I could rent a plane personally, and we wanted to limit police involvement. The cops would not want to see us depart for East Germany – two hostages and Detmer's killers. As if on cue, Inspector Van Dijk approached. "Ja, I see you talking on the telephone. A breakthrough?"

Kees quickly interjected, "A family matter."

"Ah, yes. A policeman's family always suffers for the hours and uncertainties, does it not Van Warmerdam?"

Kees nodded.

"But come, we have not checked on your house, Dr. Brown. Let us go together. Perhaps you can provide some coffee?"

From Margaret Brown's notebook #2

Hospitality

Every school child learns that the Pilgrims survived because of the hospitality and generosity of the Native Americans, but we rarely hear how hospitality was an important value in almost every tribe. Pioneer explorers and settlers from DeSoto and Coronado on down tell of lavish hospitality to the white strangers, often at great cost to the hosts.

Every ceremonial occasion provided an opportunity for lavish hospitality. In fact, in some languages the same word was used for generosity and bravery; either one was a mark of distinction.

A Kwakiutl man would give away his accumulated wealth in one blow out called a potlatch. And the Aleuts received a stranger by offering him any home in the camp; provided him food and lodging for as long as the stranger stayed; and then sent him on his way fully provisioned. Pretty impressive.

22

How do we avoid taking Van Dijk to the cottage? Honesty's the best policy? That adage hasn't gained much traction with the majority of people. Deceit, evasion, half-truths and bare-faced lies seem to be the way the world operates.

"Of course, Inspector. It would be my privilege. But first could we discuss our respective objectives further?"

"I have thought about what you said, Dr. Brown. You are right. Our first priority is to protect the living, not avenge the dead. But it is hard to remember that I am a policeman when I think of those hideous pictures of Paul. I do not trust myself to confront the men who did that to him. I visit his widow every week. I fear I will not act like a good policeman. I want only one thing and that is a few minutes alone with them in a room." His face reddened. "I want only a hammer." The dark impulses that troubled Kees' conscience didn't faze Van Dijk.

He stopped and breathed deeply and deliberately; his features relaxed. "You see the inner turmoil, Dr. Brown?"

"I do, Inspector. And you understand they have the woman and unborn children that are my whole life? The last words the kidnapper said on the phone were, 'you should think about what we are doing to your pretty lady'."

"I'm so sorry, Dr. Brown. My emotions get the better of me. Your woman and unborn children did you say? – they must be saved. I must see that as a greater victory over these savages." His face hardened. "Then I will take great satisfaction in killing them myself."

Whew. Flip . . . flop. Which Inspector Van Dijk would turn up at the critical moment?

"You're torn, but you recognize that, Inspector. I trust that you will remain a professional. I don't have the same confidence in everyone else. One hothead could ruin a rescue attempt and precipitate a tragedy."

"You are leading to a proposal, Dr. Brown?"

"I am, Inspector. I think we all know the general outline of what must be done. We have to draw these killers out and create a situation where Sally is able to get some separation from them. Then, during that brief opening, they must be killed or seriously wounded. I spoke to them a few minutes ago. It's their intention that I fly them to safety – perhaps East Germany. They'll want Sally in the plane as a means to control me. Once the airplane is in the air there's little that your people can do without killing Sally and me. However, there may be opportunities during transit to the airport."

"What you are not saying, but I think you are leading to, is that only a few of my men can be involved. Men that I trust to remain calm and unconflicted. That is hard. In a small country, you eventually know many people. Paul was known and well-liked." He paused, his features hard. "Every one of these men wants to avenge him, as do I. Who is not emotionally involved? No one. But I think your proposal deserves serious consideration. Come, let us go to your house, have some coffee, and discuss this further."

"I would love to take you to my cottage, but, at the risk of being inhospitable, I cannot."

"You cannot?"

"No. That's where the kidnappers are holding Sally."

Kees looked uncertain, half expecting Van Dijk to start shouting orders to lay siege to the cottage.

To hold Van Dijk's attention while he processed this information, I continued. "We had the building fortified. The windows are bullet resistant and behind steel bars. An outer wall of reinforced concrete was added. The doors are impenetrable. The only way to breach the cottage is with the kind of weapon that would kill everyone inside. We stored enough dried and preserved food to last two weeks. In short, our well-intentioned efforts to be secure are now backfiring."

My voice was faltering, but Kees picked up the explanation. "You see, Inspector, because of the nature of these kidnappers, they will not submit to a siege. They will torture Juffrouw Taylor and force us eventually, for humanitarian reasons, to allow them safe passage."

Thanks, Kees. Thoughts of Sally being tortured were what I was struggling to suppress. What would they do with a pregnant woman? They stripped the skin off a young man in Dhaka because he was always picking at himself.

"Well, two things are clear. First, only a surgical operation involving a few men has any chance of success. Second, I am not going to get my coffee."

This attempt at levity fell flat.

———

I tried to sleep in Kees' car with no success. As I started to drift off the memory that would bring me back to full wakefulness was the image of the line of trees we skimmed over on our first landing attempt. Even my subconscious couldn't acknowledge what might be happening to Sally?

With the first light of dawn, Kees, Van Dijk, and I scouted the routes from our cottage to the airfield. We identified three:

- There was a circuitous road, if the kidnappers went by vehicle.

- There was a direct route across fields and through a copse, but this seemed an unlikely choice for two reasons: given the limited mobility of at least one kidnapper, walking would be unattractive; and there was a 150-meter section of the route across a field where there was no cover.

- There was also the path toward the boathouse. That led into wooded cover only 20 meters from the cottage. From there it was possible to turn north, still through trees, and arrive close to the end of the runway. Thanks to the prevailing winds from the west, that was usually the departure end, but these were not usual circumstances.

Van Dijk was quick to offer his assessment. "We can place sharpshooters along all of these routes, well concealed. If the kidnappers are on foot, there is a chance. If in a vehicle it is more difficult. Since these are professionals, we should assume first that they will choose transit by car. However, there is the possibility that they will believe that is our assumption and choose another route."

"Wait." I interrupted, and held up a hand. Van Dijk had gone straight to the shootout and was ignoring our most important advantage. "It's important that they believe their presence in my cottage has not been discovered and their departure plans are unknown to anyone but me. Our first task is to reassure them that there's no immediate threat – their hideout has not been discovered and they're free to select the most convenient route."

Van Dijk's expression was that of a rebuked child. "Well, Doctor, and how do you propose we do that?"

I was afraid to say more.

Kees broke the silence. "What if you walked toward your cottage as if you were going home and believed it was unoccupied. I would drive up and call you back on some pretext."

"I can see that working, but I'd have to get close enough for the kidnappers to see me while I went into my act, but not so close they would feel they had to confront me."

"Easy to do. I will drive you to your cottage. The road is thirty meters from the door. We can converse loudly. Then you will walk toward the cottage while I answer the phone. I will shout to you that the call is something we must investigate, so you will come back to the car and we will leave."

Inspector Van Dijk rejoined the conversation. "That will work once and buy a few hours. Then what? If Dr. Brown does not return to his home they will grow suspicious."

The solution to that was evident to everyone. I had – at some point – to go home and feign surprise at finding the kidnappers there.

"I need to make a call about the money." I dialed Herr Swindel, our financial advisor at Credit Suisse in Montreux. Although rarely in his office, he had a call-forwarding system and he usually answered my calls.

"Herr Swindel? Max Brown."

"Professor Brown, how good to hear your voice after so much time. Do you wish another transfer to our branch in Amsterdam? I am sorry to report that bullion prices did not do as well as I had forecast so your portfolio, while growing, is not meeting my expectations."

I cut this off and briefed Swindel on the situation. "I need every penny, centime, and sou in my account ready for immediate transfer. You must liquidate all my holdings this morning."

Silence from the other end. This was a disaster for Herr Swindel who had, with loving attention, nurtured this portfolio. "Are you sure, Professor?"

"Herr Swindel, the lives of my beloved woman and the two babies she's carrying depend on it. I'm sure."

"Very well, Professor. I believe your holdings will cash out at between 3.7 and 3.75 million in US dollars."

The larger amount was a help, but probably not enough to satisfy the kidnappers.

"When I have instructions for routing the money I'll be in touch. And, I'm sorry. You've done a wonderful job managing the money." Swindel was silent. We hung up.

"Alright, Kees, let's try your plan to convince the killers their location is still unknown."

———

Kees pulled noisily to a stop in the gravel road in front of our cottage. We talked for a minute, I gesturing and shouting like a man at the breaking point. As I turned to walk up the path to the cottage, the car phone rang, a pre-arranged call from Van Dijk. Kees called me back – "They say maybe they have found something in Bollum" – and we drove off, gravel spewing from the tires.

The hardest part? Walking toward Sally, then walking away.

23

The best lack all conviction

Kees, Van Dijk and I went to the airport to see what was available. Work had already begun extricating the Mooney we'd borrowed the night before; it had been towed out of the marsh grass onto the taxiway where two men were cleaning it up. Sorry, Mooney. I hate to inflict pain on any airplane in the self-serving hope the planes will requite that concern.

There were two Piper Lances, one of them turbocharged; Kees phoned the airport manager and asked him to bring the keys for both. As I was checking the exterior of the turbocharged plane, a short, jowly man, the manager, joined us and introduced himself as Mijnheer Willems. No first name was supplied.

"So, ja, what do you policemen plan to do with *this* airplane? Crash it like the one last night?" The tone, a scolding schoolmarm. "This is very unusual you do not present me with official papers to inspect private property." The airport manager brought us back to a reality the events of the night had obscured. Just because evil people were doing terrible things, the normal constraints of the civilized world hadn't been suspended.

Even the experienced Van Dijk, obsessed by visions of the tortured Detmer, had, it appeared, succumbed to the same belief that any means were justified to stop the kidnappers. Neither policeman had a ready explanation so I spoke.

"Mijnheer Willems, as you are probably aware, serious crimes have been committed by four men who are now holding my pregnant partner hostage here on Ameland." How could I say those words so calmly? "These are the same men who took Dr. Juffermans and his family hostage a few months ago. They are also the same men who tortured and beheaded the policeman from Leeuwarden." The airport manager's expression didn't change. I didn't check Van Dijk's.

"Thanks to the cooperation of your tower controller last night we were able to keep the kidnappers on the island. I will, of course, pay all costs of repairing the Mooney."

Kees broke in, "We were engaged in what is called in English 'hot pursuit' – *achtervolging* in Dutch – and in such circumstances the police are allowed to commandeer private vehicles when the crime is serious and the criminals are dangerous."

"I see no hot pursuit now," observed the manager dryly.

God's gonads! I can't deal with this. Sally and the babies? And this prick is standing here with the keys in his hand and his head up his tight ass?

Kees and Van Dijk looked uncomfortable. Apparently we had been planning to operate outside the law.

"We need to set a trap," I resumed. "The kidnappers have demanded that I fly them to safety in a plane such as this one."

"That is all very well, but you cannot just take another man's aircraft without some kind of approval." The conversation over – in his view – he started to turn back toward his office at the far end of the taxiway. That was more than Van Dijk could take. His face reddening, he stepped in front of the manager and spoke to him in Dutch in a rising voice. The manager appeared unfazed by the escalating tirade.

Kees, always the level-headed one, interrupted, "Inspector, allow me a few words in English so that Dr. Brown may also understand what is being said that has such importance for the survival of his beloved woman and two unborn babies." This, of course, was to remind the sanctimonious protector of private property of the stakes.

"Willems, although I am a policeman – and we have known each other for many years on our little island – I am also a husband and a father, as are you. There are times when we must choose among our responsibilities. My responsibility to protect life is always higher than it is to protect a piece of metal. There is no question in my mind what now must be done. We must work together – we are Dutch, no? – to try to save the lives of three innocent and vulnerable people."

Try to save the lives? A more positive statement, please, Kees.

"What Dr. Brown is describing seems logical and it is the best idea we have. We must create a situation where the kidnappers feel they are about to make their escape and they will let down their guard. For this, we need an airplane because that is what the kidnappers have demanded."

"So, you will not actually take the airplane?"

Fuck yes, I'll take the airplane if it comes to that! Fortunately, Van Dijk answered for the group.

"It is our intention to lure these killers into the open where they can be captured or shot. As you can see, this airfield provides open space and few bystanders. I feel it is our best opportunity to stop these savage beasts." His face darkened again; the images of Paul Detmer were never far from his thoughts. "We will of course, also prepare to intercept them as they travel to the airfield."

"So, what is it you need from me?" Very grudgingly given.

I answered. "There can be nothing to arouse suspicion. It must look like the plane is ready to go. The kidnappers have asked me to prepare the plane and if they believe I've lied, well . . ." Shaking off the dark thoughts about the consequences of any failure, "I noticed a couple of things. First, the tanks aren't full. Can you get someone to top them off?" The airport manager nodded.

"Second, I don't see oxygen in the plane." That's not unusual because it's infrequently wanted and adds weight. "I'd like a bottle of oxygen installed and one oxygen mask with a long tube – at least two meters. If possible, put the bottle under the pilot's seat and run the tube forward up past the pilot's knee." The manager looked skeptical at this request, his first change of expression. "And then would you make sure there are a complete set of VFR sectional charts for a radius of 500 miles."

"For the oxygen we will have to bring someone from Leeuwarden. How soon will you need this?"

Kees answered. "Today. Early today. Noon." The manager started to protest but Kees waved his hand dismissively. Fatigue and anxiety will render even the courtly Constable VW impatient and curt.

The airport manager asked, his basic sourness returning "So, are there any more difficult demands you wish to make? Perhaps a beverage-service cart? Or may I proceed?" Hadn't anything sunk in with this idiot? But, dangerous to alienate the guy so I spoke first.

"No, for the moment that's all I can think of. Oh, wait. Is there any chance the owner of this plane might take it?"

Willems considered the question. "Not likely. The owner is, as you can see by the plane's registration, a South African. He only visits Holland on mining company business."

Perhaps the politics of the plane's owner figured into the manager's agreement to cooperate. "He almost never flies. This is just an expensive toy he lost interest in. However, to be sure, I will instruct the tower to prohibit movement of the aircraft." He cocked an eyebrow, daring us to make another request, then deposited the keys on the wing before resuming his waddle up the taxiway toward his office.

Kees and Van Dijk launched into an animated discussion in Dutch, presumably about the tyranny of petty bureaucrats. I spent the time in the plane, familiarizing myself with the controls and instruments. *How were those minutes passing for Sally? The helplessness.*

It was an expensive toy: leather throughout, curtains that could be pulled along the windows, the radios looked new, and the nav equipment and instruments were IFR compliant. With the airport manager out of sight, I checked the oil level and drained a little fuel from the tanks, checking for the presence of water. There wouldn't be the luxury of a thorough pre-flight later, if it came to that. I started the engine to determine if there were any quirks and to make sure the battery was good, a reasonable precaution given the plane was rarely flown. Then I took the Pilot's Operating Handbook, a great fat tome. We locked the plane and headed back to the cottage.

We all knew what was next. I had to return to my cottage. I'd probably be roughed up, there would be no turning back on our current plan, and I would see Sally and come face-to-face with what they'd done to her.

From Margaret Brown's notebook #4

Sometimes it's too much to read about!

- In 1637 700 Pequot gathered for their thanksgiving festival. In the early hours the Dutch and English ordered them out of their longhouse where they were shot or clubbed to death. The women and children who stayed inside were burned alive. The Governor of the Mass. Bay Colony declared a 'Day of Thanksgiving' because 700 unarmed people were murdered.

- After another raid on the Pequot in Stamford, Conn. another Day of Thanksgiving was declared. The heads of the Pequot were kicked like soccer balls through the streets.

- Even the friendly Wampanoag didn't escape the madness. Their chief was beheaded and his head was impaled on a pike in Plymouth, Mass where it remained on display for 24 years.

I can't comprehend such savagery.

24

The worst are full of passionate intensity

I was fumbling with the keys to the door when it swung open; two hands reached out and yanked me inside. I regained my footing and received a hard blow to the solar plexus. I pitched forward onto the floor, gasping for air. A scream located Sally. She was tied to a kitchen chair, her lip cut and her left eye swollen closed. Dried blood was on her blouse.

"Why you insane motherfucking savages!" I lurched to my feet and charged the nearest kidnapper. A sharp pain exploded in the back of my head.

Sometime later I regained consciousness. No more rash moves. Could I pretend to be out a while longer and gather information about our situation? No. I must have stirred.

"Our sleeping beauty is rejoining us. Welcome home, Professor. You are a lucky man that we want your services as a pilot. The temptation to remove you once and for all from our path is strong."

That, and the fact that you're waiting on the money.

"Your cottage is charming, Professor, and your little wife is an excellent hostess. But we don't want to overstay our welcome. Do you have the five million?"

My thoughts and vision weren't clear yet. I groaned theatrically to buy a little time to come around. And, God's ganglia! My head hurt.

"Five million cash? On me? Don't be absurd!" The nearest kidnapper swung back his foot to kick me but the one who'd been speaking stopped him.

"Patel, easy. We need the professor in good shape to fly the airplane." Patel looked disappointed. I wasn't in good shape; my eyes kept going out of focus.

"Back to the money. What arrangements have you made that would persuade me there is any reason to allow either of you to continue living?"

My head was clearing. The interrogator was trying to sound like a sophisticated movie villain. Was there some way to use that? Play to vanity?

"You sound like a man who knows something other than torture and beheading. Explain to your colleague how large amounts of money are moved around in the world today, Mr. . . .?"

"Mr. Mehta. I'm sure some quisling in RAW gave you our names already. So, I take it you were assuming the funds would be wired to an account. We weren't, but that may be the most practical option. And you have the full five million ready to go?"

"I have 3.7 million, and I've asked my financial manager to see if a loan can be arranged for the remainder. We all realize of course," scanning all four faces, "that loans are sometimes slow to come through."

Patel, who'd wanted to kick me, answered, "No. Five million or you watch this woman die. Now." *Jesus, no! Did Patel speak for the group?*

I turned to Mehta, the voice of reason – by the low standards of the gang. There were two of him; the double vision had returned. "If Sally dies, you get nothing. If I die, same. If we both die you will never get off this island alive. There are over 100 police and Marines out there. Each one is carrying a picture of the police officer you beheaded. They all want you dead, and few of them would be satisfied if it's a quick death."

Mehta motioned at a chair. I was hauled to my feet and dropped into the chair where my arms and legs were tied to the back and legs. I looked at Sally and tried to convey confidence and authority, two feelings that were absent.

Mehta smiled beneficently, then glanced wistfully at Sally. The message was clear: Her fate depended on my playing ball. He was enjoying the act.

What now? Kees and Van Dijk had debated – at length – where to place snipers, but there'd been no discussion of the rôle Sally and I might play. To the cops we were pawns: following the instructions of the kidnappers, ducking for cover when the fireworks started.

Even in my groggy state I could see we needed to get things moving; Sally looked like she was in trouble and I'd been without sleep for over 30 hours; my ability to plan and adapt was eroded by fatigue, anxiety and now a concussion. But, we couldn't move too quickly; Willems needed time to install a basic oxygen-supply system in the plane. The oxygen figured in one of several harebrained plans I'd hatched to get us out of this. Maybe a mid-afternoon departure? Some additional time for my vision to settle down would also be welcome.

"Shall we start then, Mehta, with the transfer of the 3.7 million that's available?"

Mehta motioned Kapoor and Singha, the two limpers, to join him in the bedroom to confer. Patel was left behind to monitor the hostages. Apparently his counsel wasn't highly valued within the gang.

After several minutes someone picked up the bedroom telephone and placed a call. International. Too many digits for a domestic call. A hushed conversation in German followed. Interesting; perhaps there was a learned man amongst them. That was the image Mehta was trying to project. I couldn't understand what was said, but I knew that a bevy of wire-tappers, supervised by Kees and Van Dijk, were listening in. Holland: number one in wire-tapping.

The trio emerged and Mehta checked me over, perhaps to see if Patel had snuck in a few licks during his absence.

"Tentative arrangements have been made. We will confirm shortly. And the airplane? Your other assignment?"

"I went to the airport this morning. There are only a few airplanes that hold six passengers, and of those, only two that are single-engine. I have no experience in twin-engine small aircraft. Of those two, one may have the longer range and I checked the tanks; they're full. I believe this airplane will also fly high which extends the range and might be helpful if we encounter bad weather."

"Bad weather?" Mehta looked surprised. Had these idiots assumed this was KLM? I was a fair-weather pilot, at best.

"Yes. You do understand I haven't flown for many years. One of the skills that decays quickly is flying by instruments. I'm confident I can execute simple maneuvers on instruments, but I wouldn't be able to shoot a complex approach in poor visibility and low ceilings. We need good weather at the destination."

Mehta left the room. Another international call in German. He returned.

"I have just spoken with someone at our destination. She says the weather is good now, but is expected to deteriorate this evening. The next forecast for good weather is the day after tomorrow."

I looked at Sally. She was just holding on. We needed to wrap this up soon. The news that the weather was expected to go down tonight was welcome. That meant, if we were going east, that we'd have to fly over clouds which would provide an excuse to climb. An undercast of clouds would also make it more difficult for the kidnappers to gauge our altitude. I hoped Kees and Van Dijk, who were listening in on the phone calls, had figured out the implications for the installation of the oxygen. They didn't have much time.

"There is one thing you may want me to do." Raised eyebrows. "Study the Pilot's Handbook for the plane. It would take the guess work out of the speed for takeoff, final approach, when not to extend gear and flaps, and those kinds of things."

"Why not. We are waiting on the financial arrangements. No, don't untie his hands. Patel, hold the book in front of our pilot. It will give you something to do besides hitting people."

The operating speeds were placarded in the Piper. I didn't need that. I did want to know what the operating ceiling and limitations were and I had Patel leaf through the pages. The Piper Aircraft Company boasted the plane would operate at 20,000 feet and cruise comfortably at 175 KIAS. I wasn't counting on either of those figures still being accurate. When the plane came out the factory door several years ago they could have been, but if we could get above 17,000 feet that might be enough.

"Could one of you give Sally some water? And perhaps some food?" I didn't bother to ask that she be allowed to lie down. That wouldn't be granted. The lesser limper brought a glass of milk from the refrigerator and some crackers. He slowly tilted the glass as she drank. Then he fed her the crackers. They kept her tied up. A mark of respect.

I continued to read the aircraft manual, although my vision would occasionally slip out of synch. Maximum airspeed (191 knots), positive g's (3.8), negative g's (don't pull negative g's), endurance (7 hours, but that's certainly optimistic), and so on. Somewhere in the past I'd heard that an aircraft had to be able to withstand forces 50 percent higher than those published. Can I believe that?

Patel seemed too thick to attach importance to any of the information I was looking at, but Mehta might, so whenever Mehta approached I told Patel, "Nothing there. Turn the page please."

The airport operator had now had three hours to take care of the fuel and oxygen; I assumed Van Dijk had gone back to impress on him the urgency of the situation.

The phone rang. "Answer it," Mehta ordered. I looked at him, bewildered. My hands were tied behind my back to the rungs of the chair. "Patel, hold the phone for him. Speak very carefully, Professor." Mehta brought a steak knife from the kitchen and pressed the point into Sally's distended belly. "I have never performed a Caesarean Section, but I'm willing to give it a try. Understand?"

I nodded.

"Hallo, met Max Brown." A torrent of German came out of the earpiece. I nodded at Mehta. "It's for you."

Mehta put down the knife. There was no blood. A lengthy conversation in German followed. Mehta signaled for something to write with and took down, what I guessed, would be bank account information. After a string of groveling '*danke*'s he hung up.

"Your turn with the phone Professor. Here's the information."

From what I'd learned from Herr Swindel, it looked wrong. Back during my pre-Sally days, I would visit Swindel's Montreux office to discuss the portfolio. I'd allowed him to wax indignant about the currency restrictions in place around the world; it helped extend the conversation since I had nothing else to do. On one of those occasions he'd vented on East Germany. "Everything," he fumed, "*everything* goes through the *Staatsbank* which is corrupt and does not allow citizens access to their foreign currency." Placing any impediment between a man and his money was a high crime for a Swiss banker such as Herr Swindel.

I dictated the phone number to Patel who dialed.

"Herr Swindel, Max Brown again. I have the routing information."

"And I have liquidated your holdings, Herr Professor," said with great heaviness in his voice. "The total cash on hand is now $3,761,278. To where are we sending all your money?"

"It goes to an account in the *Deutsche Außenhandelsbank* in Wismar, DDR. The account number is . . ."

Swindel interrupted, "It will never happen. All foreign currency goes only to the *Staatsbank* in East Berlin. Only very powerful people in the DDR are able to hold foreign currency."

I continued, "The account number is 000326745-1. You will have to look up the SWIFT or routing information yourself." I signaled that Patel hang up before Swindel could protest further.

"How long will this take, Mehta?"

"Professor, you are the one who sounds like an expert in international finance. SWIFT? But, what is the hurry?"

"Weather. Remember?" Mehta shook his head to convey indifference. We couldn't let this drag out; Sally's head was drooping. "I'm surprised it hasn't occurred to any of you, but at some point, there will be a knock on that door. The police or a concerned neighbor will check in on me. I grant that you have

certain assets to play, but your extraction becomes more difficult when the police and Marines know where to find you."

Mehta's expression didn't change, but he had to understand
the facts of the situation. "Alright. I want everyone to prepare.
First, we must all eat some food and drink. That includes our
two hostages. We will call a taxi as I think the walk is too much
for Kapoor to make again – last night was difficult – and we
would be recognized. Pity you do not have a car, Professor."

Sandwich meat and cheese were taken from the refrigerator
and eaten without ceremony. I was disappointed none of the
kidnappers touched the alcohol. A little impairment on their
side, to match my fatigue and unreliable vision, would be welcome.

After thirty minutes had passed, Mehta announced, "Now,
we will see if your little Swiss banker has done what was asked
of him."

Another phone call and more German. Mehta spoke little
but his face clouded.

He hung up; there'd been no '*danke*'s. "There is a complica-
tion," he announced to his three colleagues. Then he switched to
Hindi, but it was obvious from the rising tone and gestures that
Swindel had been right. The money hadn't gone through to the
account in Wismar.

"We will not be leaving today, Mr. and Mrs. Brown. The
central bank in East Germany has intercepted the money. My
contact is sure that this will be resolved in a few days, but in the
meantime, Professor, you have not delivered even the small part
you promised."

"Mehta, I've done what was in my power to do. I have delivered all of my money. I have not requested money from official sources which would have compromised you. And I am not
responsible for the policies of communist dictatorships. This is
no longer a problem which I can resolve. Given the stakes, believe me, I would if I could." Was I overplaying it here? Trying
to sound like I was an equal partner in the process?

The roar of a loud motor outside sent Singha, the lesser
limper, to the window. More Hindi.

Singha explained in English, "We almost had a visitor. A Marine armored vehicle stopped briefly out front, then left." The appearance of heavy military equipment and a near miss seemed to have surprised Mehta. He signaled to the limpers and the three retired to the bedroom to confer. Patel looked annoyed. I decided not to goad him as his range of responses seemed limited.

I looked at Sally. Her eyes were closed. Resting, I hoped. Not unconscious.

After five minutes Mehta and the other two emerged. "We will go now." He addressed Patel, "Dileep, I am sure you will agree. Our contact in Wismar says she can resolve the problem with the central bank. It is as much in her interest to do so as it is in ours. I think we should leave Holland where our security becomes less sure all the time. We will keep our hostages with us until the financial arrangements have been concluded." He turned to me, "Professor, call a taxi." To everyone, "At the risk of sounding parental, I want you all to go to the bathroom now. Yes, you too, Mrs. Brown. I will monitor, but I will be a gentleman." Irony in the direst circumstances: Mehta tortured and killed, but refrained from peeking at his captives' knickers.

Sally and I were released from our chairs and allowed use of our hands to go to the bathroom. We were also permitted some cold cuts and a long drink of water. Sally hadn't spoken yet. Would she sound better than she had on the phone? "Maxsh. I'm shorry."

"What!? Sorry?"

"I shcrewed up and let them in. They said you were hurt." *Oh, Sally, those words are killing me. We all know who set us on this path.*

"You didn't screw up. I got us into this. We'll get out, somehow." Her returning look didn't convey confidence.

Mehta handed me the phone, "A taxi, and no funny business. I will detect any attempt to send a message." He picked up the kitchen knife again and pressed the tip against Sally's stomach.

There was one taxi service on the island. It operated a mini-van so our group of six would fit. I called and scrupulously avoided saying anything that might be misinterpreted as 'funny business.'

"He said he'll be here in ten to fifteen minutes."

From Margaret Browns' notebook #3.

Treatment of captives

Often war parties would not kill captives, but take them to their villages. Since many were lost in the inter-tribal battles, war captives might be adopted into the tribe as replacements for the deceased. They would be given the name of the deceased, would assume the person's family role - even to the point of marrying his or her spouse - and learn the tribal language and customs.

Whether a captive was killed or adopted depended on the circumstances and needs of the tribe.

Since the Native Americans did not discriminate on race, a white captive could as easily receive the same treatment. That would be perplexing for the white captive.

That would be hard - going along with your captors.

25

The centre cannot hold

We were given more food, then Mehta directed Patel to tie us up again. Our legs were left untied but our hands were bound behind our backs with plastic quickstrips. There'd be no attempt to disguise the fact that we were leaving under duress. Everyone on the island was on the lookout for four Indian men, and the condition of Sally's face would erase all doubt that we weren't departing on vacation.

The promised arrival time of the taxi came and went. "They're usually late," I offered.

At twenty minutes a yellow taxi van came slowly down the gravel road and stopped in front. The driver's face was concealed by a cap as he appeared to be busy filling in a form. He honked impatiently.

"Everyone on their best behavior," said Mehta with what sounded like genuine cheerfulness. Was he one of those people who enjoys the chase?

The taxi driver jumped out of the cab and headed toward the door, looking at his watch with annoyance. God's bunions! It was Inspector Van Dijk, vying for an Oscar.

"Do you have luggage?" he shouted as Mehta cracked open the door. Van Dijk peered at Mehta. "Where are the Browns?" he asked apprehensively. "Who are you?" Van Dijk took a hesitant step backward as if the realization was dawning on him that he was face-to-face with a threat. Mehta opened his coat and pointed a pistol at Van Dijk, who froze.

"Good boy. We can all work together. Your task is a small but useful one. You will drive us to the airport. Your payment for that short ride will be the greatest you have ever received: your life." Van Dijk nodded.

Mehta organized us at the door. He and I first, a pistol digging sharply into my ribs. The two limpers next. And Patel brought Sally; she yelped when he pulled her up by her wrists which were tied behind her back. I was leaning to Van Dijk's position: a little alone time with Patel and a hammer, preferably a claw hammer.

Mehta led our procession to the cab. He casually reached through the driver's window, grabbed the microphone from the radio and threw it into the high grass on the far side of the road. Addressing Van Dijk, "You will be required to stay with us at the airport until we depart. But then, you will have little choice since we will tie you up so that we may have a head start. Only sporting, don't you think?" Mehta was back in sophisticated master criminal mode. New audience?

Van Dijk was trembling. "I have a family. Small children. I want no trouble."

"Good, good. We have always found that a devoted family man has the right priorities. He's less inclined to do something rash that transforms him from family provider to dead hero."

The van was a tight fit for seven people. I sat between the two limpers in the back seat. Sally sat with Patel in the middle row and Mehta sat in front, his pistol trained on the perspiring driver.

Thinking like a pilot for the first time all day, I noticed the sky. The cloud cover was light and high – maybe 10,000 feet. How high above that would the clouds extend? We needed to break out on top or I'd be flying instruments the entire distance. Tiring for someone out of practice. And the occasional periods of unfocused vision continued.

Van Dijk's presence was reassuring, but also ominous. What had he planned? Kees might have trusted me to solve the problems ahead, but Van Dijk would not. He gave every impression of a man who relied first on his own instincts.

Nothing rash, Van Dijk. Let's not transform anyone into a dead hero.

The van bounced along the gravel road from our cottage until it joined the hard surface of the Verbindingsweg. All the wonderful walks we'd started on that street. Sometimes in lousy weather – usually in lousy weather – but happy walks. No happiness today.

The airport tower came into sight. My apprehension mounted. The dull ache in my head, left by the concussion, increased with the tension and the double vision came back. Would that prick, Willems, have disabled the Piper to ensure we couldn't take it? Flying off with Sally and four assassins towards East Germany was an unattractive option, but when none of your options look good, you try to hang on to as many as you can.

Mehta seemed to be growing perkier by the minute. "Which airplane, Professor?" I signaled the Piper parked midway down the tie-down area and the taxi pulled up in front of it. We got out of the van, but all remained on the side of it away from the line of trees on the far side of the road.

Mehta stared at the plane, a scowl developing. "A fine looking airplane and a good one, I'm sure. But I don't like the smell of it – you choosing the plane. What else here might make the trip?"

There goes plan A. He pressed the knife into Sally's side. This was getting old. "There's a similar plane back there that I could fly."

"We'll take that," announced Mehta.

Were there snipers somewhere? I was surprised and relieved that Van Dijk hadn't made his move, but we'd been in the shadow of the van all this time. "I'll have to check to make sure it's ready to fly."

"I will accept that as a normal precaution, Professor." Mehta cut the ties on my hands. "Let me accompany you," and he slipped to my right side, keeping me between himself and the trees. There was a distinct odor of AvGas as we approached the plane. Removing the gas caps I motioned Mehta to inspect.

"Almost empty. We won't get 20 miles." The strong smell raised the possibility that someone had hastily drained these tanks. It was unusual to leave a plane with empty fuel tanks as it allowed room for condensation which resulted in water entering the engine at inopportune times. It looked like Kees and Van Dijk had taken steps to limit the kidnappers' options.

"Inconvenient. It appears we will have to take the plane you chose after all." He positioned himself on my left side, away from the trees again, as we walked back.

Patel was nervously eyeing the little plane, clutching the thick Pilot's Handbook to his chest as if proximity to the information it contained might improve his chances. Interesting. Maybe his apprehensiveness could be used later. "I will sit in front," Patel announced.

"Very well, Dileep. I propose that Mrs. Brown sit in the third row. I want maximum separation between our hostages." Mehta nodded at Sally, "If you will, Ma'am?"

Like most small low wing planes, this one had one door for passengers and that was on the right side, the side exposed to the line of trees. Sally unsteadily climbed the small step to the wing and ducked through the cabin door. Small planes are difficult to get in and out of, especially if you're eight months pregnant and your hands are tied behind your back.

"Who would like to keep her company? Ashok, why don't you climb aboard now. S.I., you and I will occupy the center row."

The two limpers headed to the plane, studying the difficult entry as they went. Mehta and Patel stayed with me beside the van. As Ashok climbed on to the wing and S.I. placed his foot on the step rifle shots cracked – maybe four. Ashok flew backward off the wing as if carried by a strong gust. S.I., who hadn't reached the wing yet, doubled over and lay still. My mind was slow to accept that two lives had been snuffed out, the victims, rag dolls lying in the short grass.

Patel was faster to figure it out. He had his gun out and, crouching, started firing into the trees when a shot sent him spinning back, his trajectory taking him into the cover provided by the van.

Van Dijk looked surprised by the attack but pulled a gun from under his jacket and was turning toward Mehta.

"Ah, I wondered as much. You are not a taxi driver. Some kind of policeman, I suppose. You will notice Mr. Policeman that I have my pistol under the professor's chin and the hammer is held back by my thumb. If I should lose control of that thumb, for any reason, a small but vital part of the professor will go flying. Please tell your men to stand down, and do it in English so I can be sure that the proper instruction is given."

Three of his men dead, and Mehta exhibited no emotion; there was no panic in his voice.

Van Dijk squinted down the barrel of his gun. "Give yourself up. You're surrounded and there's only one of you."

"Two of us," said Patel who had gotten shakily to his feet. His right hand held his pistol, trained on Van Dijk's head. The left hand held the fat Pilot's Handbook, a bullet embedded in it.

Van Dijk hesitated, then dropped his pistol and shouted in the direction of the tree line, "Hold your fire or they will kill the hostage."

Patel picked up Van Dijk's pistol, threw it out onto the field, then kicked the policeman savagely behind the knees. Van Dijk went down.

Mehta addressed the policeman. "Normally I would ask your men to show themselves, but I don't trust they all would. We must improvise.

"Patel. Go around to the other side of the plane and point your gun through the window at the head of Mrs. Brown. And Patel, please don't kill her unless it's necessary. She's our passport."

Patel ran toward the airplane, dropped and rolled under the fuselage, and came to his feet on the other side with his pistol pointed at Sally's head.

"Now you and I, Professor. Shall we board?" It was an awkward dance. Mehta kept me between him and the trees. Clumsily we mounted the step onto the wing. Mehta backed into the plane, fell into the center seat – without discharging his gun – and quickly pulled the window curtains closed. There were no clean shots left for Van Dijk's marksmen. "Professor, tell your colleagues that I now have my own gun, thumb on hammer, pressed against Mrs. Brown's forehead."

I relayed the information.

"And now, Professor, please climb in. You too, Dileep, come around." Patel did as instructed, but hesitated at the door, a curious place to stop given the rifles pointed at his back. He got in as I went through a quick check before starting the engine. We were about to find out if Willems had disconnected a wire or otherwise disabled the engine. It appeared that he saw his first duty as the protection of private property, not life.

I scanned the instruments, primed the engine, and called, "Clear prop." Why would I say that? Groping for normality? The engine came to life, oil pressure started to rise toward the green, and we pulled out onto the taxiway. So far, so good, Willems. I glanced in the direction of Van Dijk, kneeling on the grass. His arms hung limply at his sides.

As we taxied out Mehta moved to the far back seat with Sally. I hoped this wouldn't create weight-and-balance problems for the plane. I've never been especially diligent about center-of-gravity calculations on the twin rationales that, a) in my particular case the laws of physics are not rigidly enforced, and b) on the rare occasion when they are, I'm such a hot jock I could fly out of the problem. Unfortunately, recent events had punctured the belief that the universe was predisposed to cut me slack, and I knew my surviving flying skills were rudimentary. But, this didn't seem a good time to introduce delays and complications – such as the arcane science of weight-and-balance – to our captors.

We bumped along the grass taxiway. How would Patel and Mehta react to the loss of their two comrades? Would they take it out on us? Or were they mentally dividing $3.76 million by two, rather than four?

26

The plane accelerated slowly down the runway and I wondered if I'd set the trim and had the right amount of flap extended. I also wondered if Willems had jammed or disconnected the elevator. *Why attribute such despicable motives to poor Willems? Weren't the motives of our current traveling companions enough to worry about?*

The Mooney had been much peppier, but the Piper was carrying a lot of fuel and four passengers. We broke ground at around 75 KIAS. I pulled up the gear and flaps and turned right, taking us out over the North Sea. As we banked into the turn, no more than 50 feet in the air, Patel reached for the yoke, then he pulled away. This was not a confident flier. We flew north, skimming the water, for several minutes. Patel looked ashen. His breathing seemed rapid.

"Professor pilot." Mehta had moved to the center row of seats. "I'm curious about our route."

"Just trying to be cautious, Mehta." Like hell I was. "Our departure was less inconspicuous than we thought it might be." Would he accept that our interests were aligned? He's probably not that stupid, but it's worth a shot. "I thought we might stay below the radar – literally – before we turn east toward Wismar."

"We're not going to Wismar, Professor. We're going to Rostock. The bank is in Wismar. My old friends in the Stasi are in Rostock" I held up a hand to signal I needed time to process this information and fumbled with the charts.

I located Rostock. "That's another 100 miles."

"Is that a problem?"

"No, but we have to climb to a higher altitude where the plane is more efficient. That means detection."

"Any military plane that intercepts us should know who is on board, Professor. They are even less likely to shoot at us than when we were on the ground."

We turned east and started to climb. At 8,000 feet the plane entered wispy clouds. At 11,000 feet we couldn't see the coastline we'd been paralleling. I focused on the artificial horizon to keep the wings level and the plane in a steady climb. The periods of double vision were becoming less frequent and shorter.

"How much higher, Professor?"

"The higher the better. A lot of things can go wrong on this flight. I'd rather conserve fuel."

It was unlikely Mehta could read the altimeter. He'd placed his hand between the seats. I checked the skin around his fingernails. Blueness would be a sign of hypoxia, oxygen deprivation. Mehta's hand showed no such signs. Patel's did but that might be hyperventilation and not hypoxia. I turned around to check Sally. She gave me a crooked smile. Heart breaking. I'd better pull this off. There was a faint outline of blue around her lips.

Thirteen thousand and climbing at about 600 feet per minute. "Mehta, to be on the safe side we should start using oxygen. The danger zone doesn't start until much higher, but Sally's breathing for more than one and you want me reasonably alert."

I pulled up the oxygen mask and studied it. It looked like the requested 'installation' had been to throw the green O_2 bottle under the pilot's seat. The mask was a simple demand-pull system. You inhaled and a flap admitted oxygen into the mask. I put it on and played with the valve. Turning the valve counterclockwise produced pressure in the mask. When I put my heel on the section of tube that was lying on the floor, the flow of oxygen stopped.

I inhaled the oxygen for a minute, then turned to Mehta. "Here, would you put this on Sally for a while. Then you and Patel should have some also." There was now bluing around Mehta's lips. Our altitude was 16,000 feet. Mehta held the mask on Sally's face; when he removed it her color had returned to normal. Then Mehta put on the mask and I cut off the flow with my heel. "Feel better?"

"Yes, Professor, I do."

Amazing what the power of suggestion will do.

You can see where we're going with this plan. Get the two killers unconscious . . . and then? I was still working on that. If we descended – and all planes will descend sooner or later – the kidnappers would regain consciousness. Could we kill them while they were unconscious? We certainly had the motivation . . . but the means? Sally was belted in and her hands were tied behind her back. There wasn't much she could do. Could I leave the controls, find a gun, and kill both kidnappers? Tricky. And if Mehta was unconscious, who would put the oxygen mask on Sally? Her blood O_2 level was more important than anyone else's.

At 17,000 feet we broke into the clear. That made flying easier.

"Mehta, I won't say I'm sorry about your two colleagues back at the airport, but I do want to tell you that I knew nothing of that plan and would have opposed it if they'd briefed me. My only priority is to save Sally and the babies."

"Babies? Twins? You are foolish to tell me these things, Professor. My leverage just increased."

Obviously I needed more oxygen and inhaled some.

"But, yes, our fallen comrades. I am of two minds. I must tell you that they were slowing us down. I think we would have been off the island and in the clear if we did not have to help Kapoor along. I, personally, did not want him to come on this mission, but he insisted."

I inhaled more oxygen and asked Mehta to hold the mask on Sally. He did and then gave it to Patel whose skin was now graying. I stepped on the tube.

The lack of oxygen was making Mehta loquacious. "Sort of a Hammurabi's code thing, isn't it, Professor?"

"An eye for an eye?"

"Exactly. We had not intended your parents' death and you had not intended the same for Kapoor and Singha."

"Not intended my parents' deaths? You locked them in a burning building!"

"We just wanted them scared – moderate injuries. Something that would flush you out of hiding."

"Hiding? But you knew to send the press clipping to my apartment in Montreux."

"We sent over 100 press clippings. We blanketed the high-priced apartment buildings in the area." I offered Mehta the oxygen mask and, this time, let him inhale some. I wanted the rest of the story. Mehta was pleased to continue without prompting.

"Singh, for all his brilliance as an intelligence agent, was not a reliable communicator. He was the only one with a visa to Europe at the time. When the Fulbright Commission told us you were in London, he went on alone. The last contact we received was a one-line postcard from Basel that he – following you – was about to reboard a train that would stop in Lausanne, Geneva, and Montreux."

It all fell into place. Singh had tailed us from London, to Paris, to Montreux where Sally shot him. In his rush to keep up he hadn't been able to notify his gang.

"So if you didn't know we were in Montreux, how did you pick up my trail when I went back there last fall to pack up our things? You certainly were getting close to us in Utrecht."

"Ah yis. Sometimes fortune rewards the persistent, Professor. When you changed flight reservations in the Geneva airport – *after* clearing security – it set off alarms in the security and intelligence services. Singh had given your photo to one of his friends in French intelligence. The man informed us of this highly unusual event and Kapoor was waiting at Orly in Paris to see who this person was – a person that roughly matched your description – who had been taking evasive measures. It was you, struggling with large bags."

That had been me, alright. I thought I was being clever with all the jumps between names and modes of travel. All I'd accomplished was to draw attention to suspicious behavior.

"Kapoor lost you in Amsterdam when his stubborn Dutch taxi driver refused to keep up with your cab. We did know you were heading down the E35 and guessed that a person would not want to pay a cab fare further than Utrecht." Mehta sounded pleased at this particular bit of sleuthing.

I'd heard enough. The exertion of shouting over the engine's roar seemed to have reduced Mehta's blood oxygen. Were his lips bluer than before?

"Your friend is not a happy flyer, Mehta. I think he's hyperventilating – too much oxygen, ironically. You should have some yourself, however." I stepped on the tube again while Mehta inhaled deeply.

We were at 19,000 feet and it was clear the Piper would go no higher. We were staggering along at just above best rate of climb airspeed. At that moment, an F-104 rocketed by our left side. *Luftwaffe.* We were going far too slow for him to fly beside us. We were at 90 KIAS and the 104 would fall out of the sky at 150.

"I expected this," said Mehta in a distant voice. "When the aircraft markings change to DDR you will know we have crossed the border."

And what kind of reception would the East Germans give us? There was no way for Mehta to have alerted his Stasi friends of our aircraft identification. Would some DDR *Luftstreitkräfte* commander conclude we were toting a nuclear device and order us shot down? Not impossible.

I put the plane into a shallow dive and traded 300 feet for fifty knots of airspeed. The 104 made another pass, flaps down to try to match our speed. The pilot was signaling descend. *Not gonna happen, Fritz.* The clouds below looked dark and menacing; off to the southeast the orange glow of lightning lit up the grey undercast. This was the bad weather Mehta's Stasi contact had told him about. The 104 pilot repeated the gesture with increasing intensity, then he peeled off.

Mehta rotated use of the oxygen mask. The light in the sky was starting to fade. Fifteen minutes later a MiG-21 sidled up beside us. I was disappointed and a little offended they didn't care enough to send their very best. Didn't we rate a MiG-29, or at least a 23? I gave him the finger. Just like old times in 'Nam.

I needed more oxygen.

Patel appeared to be asleep. I turned to look at Mehta. He was waving at the MiG, his hand swiveling at the wrist, like British royalty. The MiG pilot tapped the side of his helmet and held up five fingers, the signal to go to 'pilot common,' radio frequency 123.45. *Not gonna happen, Hans*. My American English going out over the airwaves would alarm the *Luftstreitkräfte* and I needed to keep Mehta, our German speaker, in a vegetative state. I waved the flat of my hand fore and aft by my ear and up and down in front of my face, the US military's signal for radio failure. Were these signals universal? Then I reduced airspeed and the MiG slipped ahead of us.

"Here, Mehta, give Sally some more oxygen." He lazily did so. Was the mask held tightly enough on her face? "Mehta. Make it easy on yourself. Attach the mask to Sally's face with the elastic strap."

He looked at me questioningly, then pulled the strap behind her head. She'd be okay. Then another thought occurred: what about the pilot?

I started breathing more rapidly. Is that the right thing to do? The instruments were growing blurry. I was in trouble. If I passed out I hoped I'd come around before the airplane was torn apart by whatever maneuver it fell into. What a terrifying death for Sally.

An idea. I picked up the long oxygen tube and started gnawing on it. Tough rubber. I chewed on it. Damn! Very tough rubber. *God's ocherous incisors! Was it necessary to make the tube this strong?*

I was going under and halfway realized it. Then, I felt a little bit better. *That's alarming. Is this how it is when you check out from oxygen deprivation?* More chewing created a small hole in the tube. Clamping it between my lips, I breathed through my mouth. The world came back into focus. I looked back at Sally who shouted, 'Okay" through the mask. Patel was slumped in his seat and Mehta looked dazed. It was difficult to tell if he was conscious or not.

The MiG, unable to match our slow speed, 110 knots, was gone, probably circling around to rejoin us for another pass.

How many passes would he make before the East German *Luftstreitkräfte* command decided to elevate matters to the next level? I needed to take the initiative and deal with the immediate threat, the two killers inside the plane.

27

Forty miles east of our little cottage on Ameland is the town of Groningen, birthplace of Daniel Bernoulli who arrived in Holland – and the world – on 8 February 1700. Bernoulli wound up teaching in Switzerland and the Swiss have appropriated him, but he's Dutch. He's remembered today for the Bernoulli Principle.

Daniel observed that as a gas passes around a body it has to accelerate to complete the trip to the far side. The molecules of air, forced to move faster, thin out and the pressure exerted by this thinned out gas decreases. That's how airplanes stay aloft. As the wing races through the sky, the air that passes over the top of the curved wing has further to travel and, therefore, must accelerate – and thin out – more than the air that passes along the flat and more direct route under the wing. The upshot? There's lower pressure on top of the wing, which tugs the wing upward and, voilà, the plane flies.

The same effect occurs anywhere air has to speed up. For example, the air passing around the sides of the fuselage has to accelerate and there is an outward tug on the walls of the plane. Not a dangerous amount of outward pressure, but enough to pull an unlatched door open.

Do you see where we're going?

I looked back at my beautiful Sally, her left eye swollen shut. I looked at the unconscious savage, Patel, beside me and reached over and unlocked the cabin door. It immediately swung out 12 inches. I released Patel's seat belt and pushed him toward the partially open door where he became wedged. It seemed there was enough inward pressure on the door that it wouldn't open further without force. I kicked in right rudder and corrected with left aileron. The nose of the plane slewed to the right. The air pressure on the door was reduced and it opened another six inches. Thank you, Mr. Bernoulli.

Patel was sliding steadily out the door onto the wing when his arms started flailing, groping for something to grab on to. I picked up his left leg and pushed his lower body through the door. Some primitive survival instinct had roused Patel to wakefulness and he twisted around and got both hands on the doorsill. Would he be able to climb back in? Impossible to close the door at this speed; Bernoulli was seeing to that. How to rid the world of this abomination? In the movies this is where the bad guy starts whacking on the good guy's hands. With what?

Of course! The haphazardly installed O_2 bottle. I pulled it out from under the seat and swung it down hard on Patel's fingers. The sill was sharp and two of his fingers were severed by the blow. The damaged hand released the doorsill but he hung on with the other. I walked the rudders back and forth; the plane swayed through the air. With a scream, Patel lost his grip and slid off the wing. Reversing the side slip of the plane while reducing speed, the door moved back in and I was able to latch and lock it again.

One down, one to go.

I looked back at Sally, expecting disapproval. She shouted through the mask, "Good that the bastard was awake for the trip down!"

What a woman!

The MiG slid by again on the left, flaps down but still unable to match our slow speed. More gestures to descend. No sense in aiding the enemy; we reduced airspeed to 80 KIAS. Then I noticed the broken hose on the oxygen bottle. It had torn loose where I'd chewed the hole and didn't look like it could be reattached. We had to descend quickly. And we had the MiG to deal with. I could breathe directly from the broken hose, but only for a few minutes as the supply would deplete quickly. And that was no help to Sally. I looked back at her; her one good eye was closing; she was going under.

I inhaled the remaining oxygen deeply and tried to come up with a plan. New ideas don't spring to mind in these situations; old ones do.

Plover? But how?

The Operating Handbook had something in there about spin recovery. I hadn't bothered to read it closely, but apparently the plane would spin and, I remembered, it could lose as much as

1,000 feet in each rotation. I wanted the MiG jock to see this. A faked injury is wasted if there's no audience.

Enough time for the MiG to make the circuit. I reduced power, pulled the nose up sharply and the plane stalled. I kicked in right rudder and a little left aileron in the hope that the MiG pilot would continue to make passes on the left.

A very gratifying spin. The left wing came over the top and the plane started to rotate in a clockwise direction. How long do we want to keep this going? The world spun around dizzyingly. Then we sank into the thin clouds. *Can I pull this sucker out of a spin?* Maybe I should have been concerned about weight-and-balance. Every pilot knows that a tail-heavy load can make spin recovery impossible in some aircraft.

Our center-of-gravity was shifting constantly. Mehta, as he passed the oxygen around, had released his seat belt. Now he was being thrown around the cabin by the rotations of the plane. If he'd just hold still, I'd whack him with the O$_2$ bottle. He looked awake and panicked.

"Professor! What's happening? Is this normal?" As we descended he was going to recover fully. And he had a gun and probably a knife. And . . . *God's flaming hemorrhoids! I'd sent Patel to his final fiery reward and I let him take his gun with him!*

Let's deal with one problem at a time.

We were passing through 13,000 feet. Two more rotations and we'd be low enough to ensure adequate oxygen for Sally. But which way did we want to be heading? West, of course; out of East Germany.

A common result of a spin is that the gyros will tumble and provide erroneous indications. If they had tumbled, it would be the end for all of us. I couldn't fly without the instruments that relied on gyroscopic stabilization. The clouds were thicker and there were no visual references.

As the directional gyro swung through 200 degrees I released pressure on the yoke and kicked left rudder. The plane flew easily out of the spin. *Thank you, Lord. Thank you, William Piper.* I leveled the wings – according to the artificial horizon – and waited to see if the gyros were stable. The magnetic compass held steady at 250 degrees; we weren't in a bank. And the vertical velocity indicator posted a steady descent of 600 feet per minute which was consistent with the artificial horizon's display.

Where was Mehta? He was sitting unsteadily on the folded-down seatback behind me – looking around on the floor. For his gun? He picked something up: two finger halves.

"Professor. You are indeed tiresome." This was followed by a sigh of regret. "I need your skills as a pilot so there is little that I can do to you. But I don't think you understand the consequences of your misbehavior. Let me demonstrate. Perhaps you will behave better as a result."

He climbed into the back seat where Sally was belted in, hands pinned behind her. Mehta grabbed her hair and pulled her head back.

"So. You have told me – unwisely – that there are two fetuses growing in your woman's belly. Tell me how you think they are arranged? Side by side? Front and back? Top and bottom? Try to visualize those two little babies, Professor. It will help you with this task." I wasn't looking back, my eyes on the artificial horizon, but I imagined he was grinning.

"Hard to know how the babies are arranged, but it doesn't matter. Life is a gamble, isn't it, Professor?" I glanced back when I heard a click. He'd opened a switchblade; the blade was five inches long, or more.

"I disapprove of gratuitous violence, Professor, but sometimes there is no other way to make a point."

Sally screamed a long piercing howl of desperation and threw herself against the seat belt. She'd figured out what was next. Mehta jerked her head back.

I corrected our bank. We'd entered a descending left turn. Maybe I should crash the plane and end it as humanely for Sally and myself as possible.

"I will let you chose, Professor. Where shall I insert the knife? Right side? Left? Top? Bottom?"

Sally started screaming and thrashing again.

"You really should make a choice, Professor. It will be better for everyone if you do. I will count to five and if I have no instructions from you, then I will start inserting the knife randomly into your wife's womb and I will continue until you instruct me which fetus you want to die. Do you understand me?" He pulled Sally's coat open and lifted her sweater and shirt. Her naked belly glistened. Mehta moved his knife in a circle around Sally's abdomen.

"One . . ." barely audible over Sally's screams. The knife circled to the top. *This isn't happening.*

"Two . . ." Now the knife was at the bottom of her belly. Was there a place where a stab was likely to do the least damage? What an awful thought.

"Three . . ."

I pulled back hard on the yoke and kicked in full right rudder to pull Mehta away from Sally. How many g's could the plane take? How many g's could Mehta take? I pulled back harder; we must be approaching four g's as I felt my vision start to fade. Reflexively, I tightened my leg and stomach muscles to keep blood in the upper half of my body. Mehta wouldn't know to do that. Sally might; I'd described it when we talked about my glory days as a USAF pilot.

I released the rudder – the side forces couldn't be doing the plane good – and noticed the artificial horizon was indicating we were already in a steep climb. I pushed the yoke forward hard and we went from four positive to two negative g's. Mehta flew from the floor to the ceiling of the aircraft. Sally was quick to see her opportunity and kicked at him wildly, but ineffectually. He was beyond the reach of her feet.

"Big mistake, Professor. You don't learn." He was swinging wildly with his knife. "I'm going to cut those little babies out so you can see your children up close."

Staring at the artificial horizon, I jerked the yoke back and turned to see Mehta crash to the floor, swinging his knife at Sally as he fell. This time she landed a foot on his face and blood erupted from his mouth.

Although he was pinned to the floor by the g forces, Mehta realized he could raise an arm and he tried to strike Sally with his knife. I threw the yoke hard to the left and pushed the right rudder; he crashed against the right floor corner. I added back pressure in a steep turn to keep Mehta pinned, but he seemed to be figuring out the game.

At some point he was going to stab God's most perfect creation, and I would have failed. Then I would crash the plane.

A new, unexpected maneuver was needed if we were going to survive. Sally was doing what she could, but I had to get into the fight. I rolled out of the turn without reducing back pressure, went to full power, and the plane entered a climb. As the artificial horizon reached a 30 degree nose up attitude, I pushed the yoke forward and felt light in my seat. Zero g's. Mehta floated up from the floor and was quick to exploit his opportunity. He swung his arm back to strike hard at Sally. I jerked the throttle to idle and Mehta grabbed at and missed the back of the center seat as he floated forward. Ready for his arrival, I swung the green oxygen bottle hard over my shoulder at whatever Mehta presented. It was his nuts. How gratifying. Mehta's response was a protracted howl. Focused on the instruments I missed the details of what happened next, but the shot to Mehta's crotch had propelled him aft where Sally met him with a solid kick which spun him around and brought him back into my sphere of action. I was ready. Another crack with the metal bottle – this time to the head.

The plane had entered a steep turning dive, a consequence of pilot distraction (a favorite term of accident investigation boards). We resumed level flight. Mehta was slumped over the back of the seat Patel had occupied. I hit him on the head with the metal bottle once . . . a second time . . .Sally's voice cut through. "Max, stop. He's no threat. Fly the plane."

Good advice. We were in another spiraling descent; the altimeter read 5,600 feet. We leveled out and picked up a heading of 280 again, the reciprocal of what we'd flown from Ameland.

Some revelation is at hand

I turned on the radio – there'd been no one we'd wanted to talk to up to that point – dialed in 121.5, international emergency, and put on the headset.

"Mayday, mayday, mayday. Piper Lance Zulu Sierra India Delta Yankee approaching West German Border near Wismar. Exact position unknown. Wounded on board. Possible structural damage."

That kind of call gets a lot of attention. The sound coming out of the headset was the garble of multiple transmitters responding simultaneously.

When the babble had subsided, "This is India Delta Yankee. You're stepping on each other. One at a time." That didn't solve the problem. The babble resumed. When it died down one patient controller came through.

"Aircraft in distress. This is Rostock Center. We may have a skin paint." *Of course you do; you sent the MiG to look us over.* "You are in the airspace of the German Democratic Republic. Turn to a heading of 340 for positive radar identification and vectors to Wismar airport."

Good and bad. Good, a vector of 340 to Wismar meant we were approaching the border with West Germany. Bad, we were still over East Germany.

"Rostock Center, thanks. Say weather at Wismar."

"Current Wismar weather: ceiling 400 feet, visibility 1 mile, altimeter 30.05."

"Roger, center. Do you have an alternate? Pilot and aircraft not equipped for instrument approach."

Silence. Valuable silence as we churned toward West Germany. I increased the airspeed to 180 KIAS.

"India Delta Yankee. Enter a two-minute left holding pattern at present position. An escort aircraft will lead you to Wismar."

"Center, Delta Yankee, you're garbled. Say again."

"India Delta Yankee, Rostock Center. How do you read?"

I ignored that one.

"India Delta Yankee, how do you read?"

I allowed a minute to pass. "Rostock Center, this is India Delta Yankee transmitting in the blind."

"India Delta Yankee, Rostock center. Reading you loud and clear. Enter two-minute left holding pattern immediately. Confirm." The urgency of the request indicated we must be getting close to the border with West Germany. How much longer could they be stalled? Could they read our altitude? The MiG hadn't been seen again. I upped the ante.

"Mayday. Any station. India Delta Yankee transmitting in the blind. We are declaring an emergency. Structural damage. Limited ability to maneuver aircraft. Wounded on board. Losing altitude. Descending through 4,500 feet." I pushed the throttle forward and climbed to 7,000 feet.

And immediately regretted the false transmission. Of course they knew our altitude. I'd lied about the radio being inoperative, and now the altitude and aircraft condition. Even the dimmest in the *Luftstreitkräfte* command would have to interpret this transparent deception as evidence of unfriendly intent.

A babble of competing responses filled the headset again.

"This is Zulu Sierra India Delta Yankee. Can anybody read us?" God, that sounded pathetic. But it did seem to keep the airwaves filled. The familiar screech and squawk of multiple earnest responders. Mehta groaned. I beaned him with the metal bottle.

How much further to the border? The weather seemed to be worsening and we were bouncing around in light turbulence. It would be completely dark soon. Didn't want to blunder into a thunderstorm – there had been two lightning flashes to the south of us – and suffer actual structural damage. And my vision had gotten fluky again.

A new voice came through. "Zulu Sierra India Delta Yankee, Bremen Center. If you read on guard, go to frequency 133.8 and squawk 7700."

Bremen is in West Germany. At least we were in range of their transmitter. It seemed like bad advice to light up radar screens all over Europe with an IFF signal of 7700 – a signal that would definitely transmit our altitude. But a change of frequency couldn't hurt. I switched to 133.8.

"Bremen Center, Delta Yankee. How do you read?"

"Five by five, Delta Yankee. Say destination."

Sally, who'd been silent through all this, shouted from the back seat, "Max, sweetheart, I don't want to complicate things, but . . . I think I'm having contractions."

Oh boy.

"Requesting vectors to the nearest hospital."

"Roger, Delta Yankee. Understand medical attention needed. Be advised, all airports in your vicinity currently at or below minimums."

God's twisted testicles! Just as things were looking up.

From Margaret Brown's notebook #5

Birth preparations

As the day of the birth approached women and their families practiced rituals to ensure a safe and easy delivery. Some of them are fun to read about.

There was a Cherokee ritual intended to frighten the infant out of the womb. A female relative would shout, "Listen, little man. Get up now at once. An old woman is coming. The horrible hag is close. Get out of bed and let us run away," This would be repeated with the gender of the infant changed.

Our quick reliance on pharmaceuticals has a long history on the continent. The Mohicans made a concoction of root bark that was drunk before labor began and there were many others. Cherokee women drank an infusion of wild cherry bark to speed delivery.

28

Role conflict. Sociologists – of which I was once one – dwell on the perils of conflicting responsibilities. Family defender, avenger of evil, maybe about to become a midwife – what else? The plane started to shudder as it approached a stall. Damn! That's the other role: pilot in command. Flying in the suds requires full attention. Nose down; wings level; inhale deeply and try to get a systematic cross-check of the instruments going. A groan from the back of the plane drew my attention away from the instruments. Sally was doubled over.

"I'll free you, babe. Give me a second to get the plane trimmed up."

Crashing around while freeing Sally in the back of the long cabin would change the balance and result in a pitch up that would a) reduce airspeed, and b) the plane would drop off on a wing as I moved from one side of the cabin to the other. Normally not a big deal, but we were in the clouds and night was falling. I would have to free Sally and clamber back to the controls before the plane had entered an extreme attitude.

I experimented with the power and trim until the plane was flying hands off, at least briefly. Then, inspiration:

Mehta. He could be useful for something, if only ballast.

I released my seat belt and crawled through to the center seat. You could sense the nose was coming up and airspeed was decreasing. I hoisted Mehta's inert body up and pitched him forward onto the right front seat. He hadn't looked that heavy. The plane's nose descended, airspeed sounds went up again.

Brilliant, absolutely flipping brilliant, Max! I meant it. The self-congratulatory behavior of a man who'd gone beyond exhaustion.

I could see for the first time how Sally'd been restrained. The seatbelt was fastened and a plastic quicktie had been threaded through the buckle to make it more difficult to release. "We're going to make it, babe," and my best smile. Sally grimaced. Another contraction?

A knife, Mehta had a knife. I crawled back to the front of the cabin. The artificial horizon indicated we were in an unusual attitude, but out of the pilot's seat I couldn't interpret it quickly. Reaching over to the controls I put in right aileron and the artificial horizon went the wrong way. I corrected and the plane straightened out.

Mehta's knife was in his hand. In less pressing circumstances it would be tempting to stick it in him a few times as payback for terrorizing Sally. He'd called it a 'demonstration' that would make a person better understand the consequences of their behavior. He seemed to be a promising candidate for just such a demonstration.

One more correction to the yoke and back with Sally. The plastic was tough and it took some sawing to cut it before I could release the seatbelt. "Okay, partner. Let's move you to the front seat where I can free your hands."

I'd been so focused on releasing Sally that I'd not noticed the changing air sounds. Suddenly the plane started to shudder again, more insistently than before. A spin from this altitude would be a problem, especially with the pilot trying to clamber forward from the back seat in a gyrating cabin.

I crashed forward and dove on the yoke, pushing it in to break the stall. What attitude were we in? Were we even right side up? Barely; the plane was nose high and in a steep left bank. I shoved the yoke forward and to the right as I dropped into the pilot's seat.

"Sally, can you make it up here by yourself, or should I come help you?"

"I'm not helplesh," she said beside my ear. She turned around so I could work on the ties that bound her hands. After some fumbling with the knot she was free and rubbing her raw wrists.

"I have to say, hotshot, I've been watching how you've handled things. I see promise. I may keep you around a while longer." And she gave me a lopsided grin.

Mehta groaned. Sally requested the honor of whacking him, which she did with evident relish. After putting him out, she tied his hands behind his back, confiscated his gun, and heaved him onto the floor between the first and second row of seats, within easy whacking range.

"Now, big time Air Force pilot, put this thing down on the roof of the nearest maternity hospital and we'll see who's been kicking me in the slats for the last three months."

What a great attitude! Too bad I couldn't come through for her.

"Right. About that? Here's the situation: Center says the weather sucks in this neighborhood. It's probably better a short distance behind us in East Germany or a long distance ahead of us in Holland. You understand the pros and cons: turn around and give birth in a jail cell; plunge forward and . . ." She cocked the eyebrow over her swollen eye. "It's your call, Sal."

"Could someone lead you down to a landing? I thought I heard that under discussion with the commies."

"They could. The problem is joining up with them in this soup. Might be time consuming." The sky to the south lit up with lightning and turbulence jolted the plane. The weather was signaling it was going to be a player. I turned slightly to the north.

"I say go ahead. My mom was in labor with me for several hours. If genetics is any guide we should have time to get west of these clouds."

"Bremen Center, Delta Yankee. We have a pregnant woman on board who is in the early (I hoped) stages of labor. What's our position and our options?"

"Delta Yankee. I have a skin paint seven miles inside East Germany. You have fast-closing traffic your three o'clock. Eighteen miles, same altitude."

Scheiße! Our MiG buddy. I turned hard to the right toward the approaching aircraft to increase the closing speed. "Roger, Bremen. Are you able to determine weapons' release?"

"Affirmative, Delta Yankee. Combined closing speed 720 knots. If he's going to deploy a weapon, it should be within the next . . . we're painting two projectiles released."

"Roger, Bremen. Give me a count down by mile."

Should I alert Sally that we were about to be blown out of the sky by the East German Air Force? There wasn't a lot of time to ponder the question; the missiles were coming at us at a speed of one mile every five seconds. Bremen Center counted down their approach.

"Seven miles . . . six miles . . . five miles . . . four miles . . . three . . . . two . . . . one . . .

I shoved the yoke forward hard, forcing the nose down abruptly. Mehta bounced off the ceiling. Sally screamed. We accelerated rapidly in the dive, the airspeed needle was well past the redline. I was wincing, braced for the explosion that would tear us apart.

"Missiles passed clear. Say your status, Delta Yankee."

I pulled hard to the left, back toward West Germany, praying the little plane would see it in its own interest to put up with these demands for another few minutes.

"We're okay, center. The hostile?"

"Passing your six o'clock, one mile. Now initiating turn to the right in pursuit."

It was a foot race to the border. It wasn't possible to drop down on the deck to get below the radar. The clouds went down to ground level. But, the MiG had been traveling at over 500 knots. That means a wide turn which gave us more time to close the distance to the border. I kept the speed in the red with full power and a shallow descent. Every small bump from turbulence made me catch my breath. *Hold together, little plane.*

"Bremen, say position of hostile."

Silence . . . and more silence. The MiG should be lining up on our tail right now. If I was in my RF-101 in Vietnam we could walk away from a MiG-21.

"Delta Yankee, sorry for the delay. Hostile has broken off."

He must have been getting too close to the border to be able to make another high-speed turn without entering West German airspace. Or perhaps the *Luftstreitkräfte* command had decided we weren't enough of a threat to risk an international incident.

I slumped in my seat, to Sally's alarm. "Max, are you okay? What's happening?"

"We just tangled with the reds' Red Baron, but it looks like it's over."

Her expression of alarm turned to one of pain as she doubled over. "It's a strong one," she groaned.

"Bremen, we're breathing easier." Actually, Sally wasn't; she'd started the measured breathing we'd practiced in birthing class. "Give us our position and options."

"Roger, Delta Yankee. You're still one mile inside East German airspace."

Turning to Sally, "You'll notice, he didn't have much to say about options. But one mile is good. We're going three miles a minute so we're probably inhaling the decadent free-market air of bourgeois capitalism already."

I traded some of our no longer needed airspeed for altitude, turned on the transponder, and set it to 7700, the international emergency code.

"India Delta Yankee, Bremen Center. We're picking up an emergency squawk 18 miles southeast of Lubeck. Radar contact confirmed."

We flew on in silence. I patted the plane's instrument panel in gratitude and watched Sally out of the corner of my eye. Her battered face contorted in a grimace and I checked the clock. Three minutes and twelve seconds later she grimaced again. Was that bad or good? She spoke,

"I wish Mehta would show some sign of life."

"Are you worried about him? You shouldn't because he's a ruthless, savage, mother- . . ."

"No. I want to pound on someone right now. Especially a man."

The radio came to life. "India Delta Yankee. Bremen Center. We have pireps of icing between 3,800 and 5,400 feet."

"Pireps?" asked Sally.

"Short for pilot reports. We're okay at 6,000 feet. Descending through that band of icing would have to be done quickly before too much accumulates on the wings. The ice weighs down the plane and it also changes the shape of the wing – usually resulting in less lift." I didn't know if these lessons in aerodynamics were diverting or annoying.

"Center, are there any fields reporting a 1,000-foot ceiling and decent visibility?"

"Negative, Delta Yankee. Low dew-point spreads have the visibility down to one-quarter mile."

"Do you want me to explain dew-point spreads?" I asked, looking for another diversion.

"No, but I'd like to paste that fucker behind the seats again," and she smacked the green oxygen bottle menacingly in her palm. Mehta didn't stir.

"Bremen Center. What's the closest airport reporting VFR?"

"Eindhoven, in southern Holland, but Groningen should be clearing up by the time you arrive."

"Holland? Max, I want to go back to Holland. I want to go to Ameland and have our babies there. I can make it." This was said with determination, not conviction.

"I want that too, babe, but that's an unlit field. Kees and I pretty much crashed there last night, and I'm expecting this to be a tougher airplane to land. The nose sits high when it's on the ground. Poor visibility in the flare."

How was she taking that disappointment? Hell, I was the pilot. We call the shots in the air. "Center, distance and course to Groningen?"

"Roger, Delta Yankee. Fly heading 258 direct to Groningen. Distance 178 nautical miles."

"Hear that, Sally? Just one hour to Groningen."

"Are you sure we can't make it to Ameland?"

God's great obdurate ovaries! This nesting/homing thing is out of control.

"We'd crash. I know you wanted home delivery, in our bed. Maybe you can do that with the next set of twins."

Men, there are times when any attempt at levity will be poorly received. Labor is one of them.

She bent forward with another contraction, but was able to stammer, "The only twins I'm thinking about are your nuts, and they're coming off! I'm not doing this again!"

I put the headset back on, as if I'd detected a faint message. "Bremen Center, can you calculate a time en route for us?"

"Roger, Delta Yankee." After a pause. "At current ground speed, estimate 62 minutes." I eased the throttle forward again, hoping fuel wouldn't become a problem.

"Max, did I hear 62 minutes?"

"Yeah. Not so bad. You know, you're still three weeks from the due date. This could just be false labor. Nothing to worry about."

"So one would like to think." Mehta stirred but Sally didn't hit him. "My water just broke."

From Margaret Brown's notebook #1.

The joyous event.
There are a few descriptions of unattended
births, but most of the accounts describe births
that were attended by a midwife and other
close family members. Men were rarely allowed
in the delivery room, and they were never al-
lowed to see the actual birth take place. A
woman in labor stood, knelt, or sat, but she
never gave birth lying down. Usually no one
bothered to catch the baby, who fell onto a bed
of leaves placed beneath the mother.

29

With the ex-RAW thugs and East German Air Force out of the way, a new enemy took their place. The adrenalin of the fight ebbed and the effect of long sleepless hours crept into the cabin. Even Sally's latest bulletin was able to arrest the encroaching drowsiness.

The clouds became thinner and by the time we were handed off to Maastricht Center an occasional ground light could be seen through a break in the clouds. I watched for those, hoping they'd somehow prove interesting enough to keep me alert. I checked the fuel gauges frequently, again trying to focus on anything that would hold attention.

A glance over at Sally's lap to see what was going on. A tiny naked infant on the floor? No. Fatigue was making me hallucinate. Sally shook me – I must have looked like I was dozing off at the controls – and then she got another opportunity to clock Mehta with the oxygen bottle.

The steady roar of the 300 horse Lycoming was hypnotic. *The familiarity of a cockpit. I do love to fly. Magical machines, aren't they? The roar of the Lycoming became a purr. I wonder if any of my asshole-buddies from the 76th are still flying. Are they great sticks like I am?*

"Ouch! Holy shit, Sally, why'd you hit my head? It already hurts like hell!"

"You drifted off and I couldn't wake you by shaking. Jesus, Max, don't screw this up now. Survive the bad guys and then kill us both just to sneak in a little shuteye?"

Scary. The hit to the head brought me back to my senses, but also dislodged something in my eyes which again refused to point in the same direction. I closed one eye to get a reading on the instruments. We'd lost five hundred feet and slipped into a left bank.

I alternated eyes. They seemed to be getting better; then worse. It was mainly fatigue, but could I trust what I saw? Sally chatted a little to keep me awake, but it was almost as relaxing as the sound of the engine. Her contractions seemed to be getting more frequent and intense. When she doubled over, it was for at least a minute. I pushed the throttle forward to the wall. *We've come too far to lose it all now.*

Twenty minutes out, more to keep myself awake than to distract Sally from the contractions, I started, "An interesting fact about Groningen. It's the birthplace of Daniel Bernoulli, who was . . ."

"Can it, flyboy."

Five minutes and fifteen miles passed. I slapped my face hard from time to time.

Sally watched me repeat this and decided a pep talk was in order. "Max, I love you very much. You're a much better person than you think you are. You're thoughtful, brave and creative. It looks like you've taken a disaster today and turned it around. I'm expecting a ticker-tape parade when we get back to Ameland."

"Well . . . uh. Thank you, but . . ."

"Let me finish!" Said with some heat. "I'm telling you this because I have a pretty clear sense of where my feelings are headed. Right now my dominant thought is about all the blithe assurances you gave me that you'd been the unfortunate victim of what you called an 'involuntary vasectomy.' If I had Mehta's knife I just might finish that job."

That statement did raise my level of alertness.

Mehta, perhaps hearing his name, groaned, which was the signal for Sally to crown him again. It seemed to help her.

"How far apart are the contractions?" Every man does this. When the conversation is going sour, he tries to change the topic.

"Just under two minutes, but you're not going to derail me that easily, pretty boy. We need to talk about taking responsibility, and being sure about things before you . . ." The radio interrupted her.

"India Delta Yankee, contact Groningen Approach on 120.3." *The Lord does love me. He sent his angels down to the air traffic control center to pull me out of an unpleasant discus-*

sion. I've never been very good at defending myself and 42 sleepless hours weren't a help.

"Delta Yankee, roger."

I gave Sally an apologetic look that was intended to signal I'd be back to her and her concerns, just as soon as this little bit of aviation business had been attended to. I switched frequencies.

"Groningen Approach. India Delta Yankee, descending though 5,500."

"Roger, Delta Yankee. Current position 27 miles east-northeast of the field. Wind 260 at 7. Altimeter 30.06. Expect runway 23."

"Oh God, Max. This is a strong one." She was doubled forward.

"Approach. You are aware that we have a woman in advanced stages of labor on board?"

"Affirmative. Medical personnel are already at the airport."

I pushed the nose down another degree without reducing power and the airspeed crept past the red line. *We are actually going to make it, if I don't fuck up the landing and the plane holds together.*

"Approach, also be advised we have a wanted criminal on board."

"Roger, Delta Yankee. There are police waiting to take custody of the criminals." They didn't know we'd already airmailed Patel off to find his own justice.

"Let's breathe together." And I started puffing; maybe that would help me stay alert. The last contraction had taken the fight out of Sally and she started breathing in time. This occupied us from 5,000 down to 2,500 feet.

"Delta Yankee, contact tower 118.7."

"Babe, I'm going to have to focus on getting us on the ground. Keep up the breathing." She grunted. Another contraction.

With the clouds behind us, the ground was covered with lights; I couldn't pick out the airport. Holland's a crowded country.

Lost at night? Circling until fuel exhaustion? That's no way to end this. We passed though wisps of cloud. "Groningen Tower, India Delta Yankee. Request vectors to final."

"Roger, Delta Yankee. Turn right to a heading of 290. The airport will be at your 11 o'clock." We'd strayed south of course. My vision remained unreliable and so was my ability to focus mentally.

Two minutes later I thought I saw the rotating beacon, but all the lights looked the same. Hard to pick these out when the city grows out around an airport. The tower turned us onto final, the long parallel runway lights pulling us forward. We were coming in fast and high. I hoped this plane slowed better than the Mooney.

It did. Airspeed was below 129 KIAS. Gear down. Green light. *Really need to snap out of it and focus.* At 105 I extended half flaps. We were high so we went to full flaps. Given the nose-high posture of the plane on the ground, I expected to lose sight of the runway over the cowling during round out. *Slipping back into the rhythm. It's almost automatic. Damn, I'm good! I hope.*

We flew down the glide slope provided by the VASI lights at the recommended 95 knots. Why so fast, Piper Company? As I recalled, touchdown was at 60 knots which left a lot of airspeed to bleed off while trying to coast along a constant few feet above the runway (on a dark night, in an unfamiliar airplane). The altimeter showed us at 300 feet. 200 feet. *Maybe I'm not so good anymore. People crash and die in these situations.* 100 feet. I felt my shoulders rise with tension and I forced them down. Easing the power back I trimmed nose-up as airspeed bled off. *Why worry? Am I not God's Gift to Aviation?*

For all of its other virtues, the Lance doesn't provide a good forward view during landing. We'd passed over the numbers on the end of the runway. *Had I rounded out too high? Would we pancake in and send airplane parts skittering out across the field? Where is the fucking runway? Where, oh where . . . ?*

Ouch! There. All three wheels touched down simultaneously. I chopped the power and tried not to balloon back into the air. Apparently that meant I eased the yoke forward, adding pressure on the nose wheel as I applied brakes.

The next part is embarrassing.

Amidst a shower of sparks, the nose gear collapsed, the prop hit the runway, the engine stopped, and Sally screamed. All in less time than it took you to read that sentence.

And flashbulbs went off. There was a large contingent of press on hand, alerted by our transmissions on the emergency frequency.

There sat God's Own Gift to Aviation. Aside from the bailout due to a bird strike in 'Nam, never a mark on my record. And there I sat on the edge of runway 23 at the controls of a wreck while the cameras rolled. Not standing on the wing, arms up in triumph. No ticker tape in Max's future.

An ambulance skidded to a stop beside the plane and two men in white dashed over, wrenched the door open, and helped Sally out. They eased her onto a gurney and wheeled her toward the ambulance.

A large black chopper settled in front of us, engulfed in a cloud of dust and debris that obscured it. As the dust cleared five people leapt out and headed toward the plane. I recognized the leader's walk.

"Good evening, Inspector Van Dijk. I'm flattered you've come to welcome us."

"Yes, Dr. Brown, and to collect the two kidnappers."

"Only one. The other made quite a splash in East Germany." God's groaning goiter! I was talking like the punch lines in a James Bond movie. "Excuse that. I've been awake a long time and trying to escape into an alternate reality where I haven't just crashed an innocent little airplane." Van Dijk raised a questioning eyebrow. "I shoved the other kidnapper out the door at 19,000 feet."

The policeman appraised me carefully. Respect? Disdain? Regret that he hadn't been allowed to do it?

"And, yes, he was wide awake as he fell." It looked like Van Dijk was suppressing a smile.

"Ja, wel. I will take the other to face Her Majesty's justice." A nod to his retinue; the four men in black pulled Mehta from the plane and dragged his limp body to a police van. Van Dijk watched impassively, then returned his attention to me. "You must join Miss Taylor in the ambulance."

Sally's gurney had been locked down in the ambulance; her head was swiveling. Looking for me? She had a limited field of vision, with one eye out of commission. "I'm here, babe." She grabbed my hand and squeezed while I winced with pain. "Hey. Shouldn't we be getting this thing moving?"

"We were only waiting for you." It was Juffermans. Old home week. Kees had to be close at hand, and he was, accompanied by Bomers and the redoubtable Nurse Marjolein.

"We'll follow. It looks crowded."

The doors slammed shut and the ambulance lurched forward, siren wailing.

30

If you're ever in Groningen and find you need to give birth, you can do worse than drop in at the Martini Ziekenhuis. It was the hospital nearest the airport and we arrived sooner than expected. Sooner than expected by me; not by the hospital. There was a large reception party at the emergency entrance waiting for Sally. Do they throw a big do for everyone or were we celebrities? Probably the latter. The press vans rolled in on our heels; journalists tumbled out and rushed the gurney. I knew Sally would be pissed when she saw the pictures; the photographers were jostling to get close ups of the battered left side of her beautiful face.

I was handed a cap and sterile gown as our parade churned through the halls. A sharp left turn and through the swinging doors into the birthing room. Juffermans, who'd been at the forefront, fell back. That fine, decent, approachable physician – although I'm not forgiving him for the two dry months – would be replaced by an arrogant specialist who successfully ignored every request made to him on Sally's behalf during the next ninety minutes.

At the conclusion of which, two very small baby girls appeared, seven minutes apart, and set up an unholy racket.

An assistant nurse brought around a tray of *muisjes* – aniseeds and sugar on a wafer – which are the traditional Dutch treat to celebrate the arrival of newborns in Holland. The obstetrician stood waiting for congratulations; his contribution seemed even smaller than mine so I hugged Juffermans and babbled my deepest gratitude. I really was grateful to the man, but the effusiveness did have something to do with spite for the specialist.

The new Taylor-Browns were placed in plastic bubbles. Oxygen? They'd had a rough trip. I followed Sally's rolling bed to a private room on the same floor. Kissed the crookedly beaming mother – she now had a compression bandage on the eye – plopped down in a chair next to her bed. And was out.

When I awoke the sun was up, people were coming and going, Sally was trying to nurse one of our daughters, and Kees was nervously cradling the other – the little package lost in his arms – tears in the big, kind policeman's eyes.

Inspector Van Dijk appeared shortly after noon. I was hoping he'd show up; Sally had never formally met the man. He apologized for the botched ambush at the Ameland airport. A trigger-happy sharpshooter had disobeyed instructions to wait until clean shots could be made on all four kidnappers simultaneously. The kid had decided that the opportunity wouldn't come and took out Kapoor and Singha. Another sniper, trying to catch up with events, put a slug in the Handbook Patel was holding; he'd been planning a head shot.

"Ja, wel. The young man will spend twelve months putting citations on improperly parked vehicles in Leeuwarden."

"Say, Inspector. Where did you lock up Mehta after you took him off our hands last night?"

"Well, I thought he would be more secure in the large national prison south of Amsterdam, even though the trip is longer. I made a mistake in that. Regrettably, the man died of his injuries during the journey."

Not injuries Sally or I had inflicted. I hope Van Dijk didn't actually use a hammer.

Kees, Van Dijk, Bomers and I stood at the nursery window, admiring the plastic bubbles that contained my not visible daughters. I'm sure they'll be the most beautiful women in the world. Although that brings another set of problems for a father, doesn't it. Nevertheless, a good start; they had their mother's red hair.

I became aware of the reflection of my own haggard face in the glass. The face of a father. *I promise you one thing my precious girls: I will never ask you to end my life.*

Epilogue

At the conclusion of the previous book I wrote that an epilogue would be premature. I hope not this time. I'd like to close this off. Enough drama for Maxwell Smythe Brown IV and his lovely wife, Sally Taylor-Brown.

Correct. We got married. A festive outdoor ceremony on Ameland attended by half of the island's 3,000 residents. The bride and groom were eclipsed by Margaret David and Mary Ralph – a mash-up of our parents' names – who drew *all* the attention.

We didn't mind the large and largely uninvited turnout. These were the people who'd turned out uninvited to look for Sally the night she was kidnapped. And, we could afford it. Crafty Herr Swindel had made a Conditional Payment to the Wismar account; the Condition that had to be satisfied was our safe release. With consummate reluctance, and after three weeks of foot-dragging, the *Staatsbank* acknowledged cancellation of the transfer. Even the East Germans don't defy the wishes of Swiss bankers.

The money arrived just in time. We had other expenses. Two thousand guilders to clean up the Mooney and repair the prop, eight thousand guilders to repair the Piper and get a thorough check of its structure, and five hundred thousand dollars into the fund created by the police for Paul Detmer's widow and children.

We were celebrities for a while. In the immediate aftermath we were the top news story in the Netherlands. And guess what? Every fucking single goddamned story included a video or picture of me crashing the airplane. I was the guy who saved the day . . . and botched the landing. So, that's me, Max Brown, the man whose sperm would not be denied, who, through determination and ingenuity saved the woman he loves, but is best remembered as the doofus who dinged a perfectly good airplane, a plane that had stood up to rough handling, a plane that deserved better. Ah, well.

My fifteen minutes of fame were further foreshortened by a zealous journalist who unearthed meteorological data on the incidence of lightning strikes along our flight path. He argued that my artful dodge of the two heat-seeking missiles had nothing to do with our survival. The missiles had opted for the more attractive $53,000^0$ F lightning over the piddling $1,300^0$ emitted by the plane's exhaust stack. That does seem more plausible. All that acknowledged, in parting –

To my asshole-buddies from our Air Force days, three messages:

    1. My wife is far better than yours. In *every* way.

    2. I have more money than any of you will ever see. And,

    3. For consolation, see below. I hope it makes you feel better about yourselves. I can afford the gesture.

Glossary

The glossary in the earlier book was found useful by at least a few readers, so, here's another.

AIVD. *Algemene Inlichtingen- en Veiligheidsdienst.* Dutch for General Intelligence and Security Service. The AIVD is primarily responsible for domestic intelligence work; the military intel service (MIVD) is responsible for international intelligence. The knock against AIVD is that they have been obsessed with reds-under-their-beds and have paid comparatively little attention to right-wing radicals and Islamic extremists. This fear of the left went so far that they created the *Marxist-Leninist Party of the Netherlands*, presumably to see who might apply for membership. They were also caught spying on the royal family. Nice work, guys.

Center. This is the air traffic control service for aircraft once they've left the immediate vicinity of an airport. Around an airport traffic is controlled by the tower and approach/departure control. There are many 'Centers', each one bearing the name of a large city within the Center's area; in the US there are 22.

"Clear prop." Pretty obvious, I hope. Pilots of propeller aircraft shout this before starting the engine against the possibility some knucklehead is crouching out of sight near the propeller.

DDR. Abbreviation for *Deutsche Demokratische Republik*, German Democratic Republic, East Germany.

Dutch pronunciation. The letters *ij* are pronounced eye; *Dijk* is pronounced dike – which is what it means. The letters *ee* are pronounced like a long a; *Kees* is case. The letters *w* and *v* are pronounced (to my uneducated ear) the same, both as v in English. (A Netherlander might disagree. The Dutch are lovely and tolerant people in almost all regards, but still delight in pointing out imperceptible – to the Anglo ear – distinctions in the pronunciation of their language.) The Dutch *j* is pronounced like an English y, so *ja wel* is yah vell, which means, unsurprisingly, 'yes, well'. The phrase is usually drawn out to signal that the speaker is either reflecting on what you've said, or – more likely – doesn't actually agree with you, but is ready to move the conversation along.

F-104. A very hot single engine fighter built by Lockheed. Also very crash prone. The Luftwaffe lost 30 percent of their 104's, taking 110 pilots to their final reward. Lockheed's marketing people wanted the thing called the *Starfighter*, but American pilots called it the *Zipper*. As the body count climbed, the German public came to call it the *Flying Coffin* (*Fliegender Sarg*), *Widowmaker* (*Witwenmacher*), and *Ground Nail* (*Erdnagel*). The Canadians, not to be left out of this race to the most macabre, dubbed their version the *Lawn Dart*. The picture at the right should provide all the evidence you need regarding the plane's popularity with pilots. Who wouldn't want to fly that?

Five by five. The clarity (the first number) and strength (the second number) of a radio transmission. One is the lowest on the scale; five by five means a clear and strong signal.

g forces. Multiples of the force of gravity. Most people are unpleasantly surprised by a force double that of normal gravity (2 g's), although this is required to make a level turn at 60 degrees of bank – not an unusual maneuver. An unprepared person will experience dimming vision at 2 g's as blood is pulled toward the feet. It's a simple matter to keep blood in the upper part of the body by contracting muscles in the legs and abdomen. When flying high performance jets in the Air Force we routinely pulled 5 – 6 g's every day. This is not by way of boasting; tens of thousands of pilots do it.

Guilder. Currency of Holland. The Dutch guilder was trading at around 3.2 guilders to one US dollar in the mid-80s.

Gyros. These are rapidly turning small wheels, much like a spinning top, that – because they're spinning – resist any attempt to change their orientation as might occur by turning or climbing or diving the plane. If you've pushed on a spinning top you've seen the effect; they resist any deviation. Ideally, the gyro maintains the same orientation while the plane moves around it (nose up, nose down, banking) and the instruments reflect that stability. A gyro can be pushed too far and tumble. Again, think of the top; you've certainly tumbled one by nudging it too hard.

Hammurabi. The Babylonian king best remembered for the set of laws promulgated during his reign. Punishments were harsh and there was no allowance for extenuating circumstances, but the code was published in the commonly used language of the street and was the first to embody the presumption of innocence.

Hypoxia. Insufficient oxygen in the bloodstream which can result in drowsiness, impaired judgment, visual impairment, and unconsciousness. Hypoxia can kick in anywhere above 10,000' and most people will start to experience some symptoms by 13,000' although acclimatization is possible over time; some idiots scale Mount Everest (29,029') without auxiliary oxygen.

IFF. A transmitter, in an aircraft, that sends out a signal read by radar scopes. The signal accomplishes two things: 1) It greatly enlarges the blip on the radarscope. 2) It can transmit any of several thousand possible signals so each plane can be assigned its own unique marker on the scope. When mode C is activated it transmits the plane's altitude. IFF stands for Identification Friend or Foe, a holdover from World War II when it was developed. This is inaccurate; the device allows identification of friends, but not foes.

IFR. Instrument flight rules. These are the regulations and procedures that must be followed when the weather is bad. The letters have become synonymous with poor flying weather, such as "Center, we're currently in IFR conditions."

Juffrouw. Dutch for Miss or Ms.

KIAS. Knots indicated airspeed. This is the speed that is displayed in the airplane. It's usually different from *true* airspeed and *ground* speed. True airspeed will vary from indicated airspeed when the density of the air rushing over the wings differs from a standard sea level condition. As you climb the air becomes thinner, and presses less firmly on the gizmos that register airspeed. As a rule of thumb, true airspeed increases over indicated airspeed by two percent for every thousand feet of altitude. The *ground* speed of the aircraft is affected by winds the airplane encounters in flight.

Klimmen. Dutch for climb.

Luftstreitkräfte. Air Force. The name was used as far back as World War I. It was retained by East Germany while West Germany adopted . . .

Luftwaffe. The West German Air Force. *Waffe* actually means weapon.

Lycoming. A US company that manufactures piston engines for small planes. The company started life making sewing machines. That isn't comforting.

Mengel. Josef Mengele was a German SS officer and medical doctor in the Auschwitz concentration camp where he conducted inhumane experiments on prisoners and was on the panel of doctors that selected which arrivals would be sent immediately to the gas chambers. Mossad pursued him for years in Argentina and Brazil, but never caught up.

Mevrouw. Dutch for Mrs.

MiG. A Russian/Soviet manufacturer of fighter aircraft. East Germany had lots of MiG-21s (claimed top speed Mach 1.5) and a handful of Mig-23s (Mach 2.2, claimed) and Mig-29s (Mach 2.25, claimed). Mach is the ratio of the aircraft's speed to the speed at which sound travels. The speed of sound depends on the medium (sound travels 4.3 times faster through water than through air, for example) and the temperature. Lower temperatures result in lower speeds. Since temperatures decline as altitude increases, the speed at which sound travels also drops as you climb. At sea level Mach 1.0 is 761 mph. By the time you reach 30,000 feet where the temperature is a nippy -53° F sound travels at only 673 mph. Am I telling you more than you wanted to know?

Mijnheer. Dutch for Mr.

O$_2$. Oxygen.

RF-101C. A reconnaissance plane produced by McDonnell for the Air Force. The manufacturer and Air Force christened the plane *Voodoo*. As always, the pilots ignored the wishes of the marketing people and called it *Longbird* and *One-oh-wonder*. I was very fond of that plane. It brought me back safely again and again, downed only once, and that by a flock of pigeons. The picture shows an RF-101C hastily departing Thanh Hoa Bridge. We visited Thanh Hoa often; it took over 100 raids to destroy it.

Scheiße. German for 'shit.' You probably knew that already. The letter *ß* is transliterated as a double s.

Staatsbank. The central bank of East Germany.

Stasi. A shortened form of *Staatssicherheit*; literally translated from German: State Security. This was the East German internal security service and was regarded as both effective and brutal. It was also immense. The Stasi employed over 274,000 and, by one estimate, counted on another half million informants. That large an espionage agency can accumulate a lot of information and the files reached a running length of 150 kilometers of shelf space.

SWIFT. The Society for Worldwide Interbank Financial Telecommunication is a network that communicates financial transactions. Each member financial institution is assigned a unique address for electronic transfers. The SWIFT code for the *Deutsche Außenhandelsbank* in Wismar was RZSB IT 2B.

The Numbers. The magnetic orientation of a runway is marked in large numbers (minus the last digit) at the approach end. Runway 23 at Groningen has a heading of 230 degrees, approximately southwest.

Transponder. A portmanteau of transmitter-responder. See **IFF**.

Trim. As the airplane changes speed, the angle required for level flight also changes; the slower the speed, the higher the nose. That angle is controlled by the elevator (the moveable horizontal surface of the tail). There are various mechanisms to hold the elevator in the desired position that minimize the pressure the pilot has to exert; the general term for these mechanisms is 'trim'.

VASI. Visual Approach Slope Indicator. These lights are placed by the normal touchdown point on the runway. If they're white, you're coming in above the recommended glide path. If red, you're low.

VFR. Visual flight rules. The regulations and procedures that apply to flight in good weather conditions. Basically: stay well clear of clouds.

Yoke. On most non-military airplanes bank is controlled by rotating the yoke and pitch by moving it forward and backward. The alternative to the yoke is a stick affixed to the floor that moves in two dimensions.

Ziekenhuis. Dutch for hospital.

Michael Bernhart was an Air Force pilot who, in younger years, barreled through the skies in exciting supersonic jets at taxpayer expense. Now, several decades later, he flies a vintage Mooney – at his own expense – to and from his writing retreat in north Georgia, and, on a weekly basis, he ferries patients who need specialized medical care to distant facilities.

Dr. Bernhart is firm in his belief that he's God's Gift to Aviation and he has never – as of this writing – harmed an airplane. That affection and concern for these magical machines has been requited.

The intrepid young warrior (1964).

www.ingramcontent.com/pod-product-compliance
Lightning Source LLC
Chambersburg PA
CBHW050032180626
46810CB00002B/679